DIVIDED: BOOK ELEVEN OF BEYOND THESE WALLS

A POST-APOCALYPTIC SURVIVAL THRILLER

MICHAEL ROBERTSON

EDITED AND COVER BY ...

To contact Michael, please email:
subscribers@michaelrobertson.co.uk

Edited by:

Pauline Nolet - http://www.paulinenolet.com

Cover design by Dusty Crosley - https://www.deviantart.com/dustycrosley

COPYRIGHT

Divided: Book eleven of Beyond These Walls

Michael Robertson

CHAPTER 1

Joni leaned forwards, but the damn thing wouldn't go any faster. The chilly wind stung her face, and her hair dragged out behind her. Thirty-one miles per hour. Quick, but not quick enough. The wheeled trailer behind slowed her down. Weighted with two bodies. They were just boys, but they were as heavy as men.

Her device told her their surroundings were clear, but she still checked every road and alley. Why rely on technology when you could look for yourself?

About ten miles from her home. They'd just passed the halfway point. The edges of her eyes burned, sore from the frigid headwind.

"What are you doing with us? Where are we going?"

Joni spoke to herself through clenched teeth. "He needs to keep his mouth shut. If they find Joni, this will all be over."

"Let us go!"

"Joni needs to shut him up."

The rubber tyres hummed against the rough concrete.

"Help!"

Joni's knuckles ached. A tight grip on the throttle. "At

least the other one is still unconscious. Or dead. Have his injuries gotten the better of him? Should Joni check? Throw him out? Lighten the load?"

Fifty-foot-tall steel walls on either side of the main road. Smaller streets branched off it. The acoustics changed with the frequent openings. *Thwip, thwip, thwip.* Her head spun from checking down each one.

Still clear in every road. White lines. No lights. Grey steel. No watching eyes. No drones. No dogs. No guards. *Thwip, thwip, thwip.* The tracker backed up what she saw. Nothing to concern herself with. She remained on the wide main road. "And why wouldn't Joni take the most direct route? The sooner she got home, the better. She took the back roads through necessity, not choice."

"Let us go!"

Joni gripped harder on the throttle. Not that it made a difference. They were going as fast as the wheeled board would carry them. "Just get him home. Get them all home. Get him home, shut him up, lock him up, cut him up. No." She shook her head. "No. Just shut him up."

"Let us go!"

"Will you shut up!" The force of her scream hurt her throat. Stars floated in her vision. Her head spun. The board wobbled. It snapped one way and then the other. She wrestled back control. "Shut up or Joni will crash. How will she get you back then?"

Joni gasped and wobbled again. A dot on her tracker. "Far away." Her heart pounded. She nodded. "They're still far enough away. Nothing to fear. We'll be long gone." She leaned left and aimed them towards one of the smaller paths.

The dot picked up speed and closed in on their location.

"What are you doing with us?"

"He really needs to be quiet. Joni can do most of the heavy lifting, but if he blows their cover ... Just shut up. Shut up now. But he can't hear her. Too far back. Maybe she should cut her losses. Maybe they didn't deserve to get taken back to Joni's place? Cut the cord. Leave the trailer with both of them strapped to it. An offering to the gods. To the guards. Same thing. Certainly in their minds."

Joni took a ninety-degree left turn into a narrower road. The closer walls amplified the whine of her electric engine. The hum of rubber tyres against concrete. Over thirty miles per hour. But, for all the noise made by their momentum, he shouted louder.

"Help! Help!"

"What does he think Joni's doing? And this is how he repays her generosity? He'll give them away. Shut up! Shut up!"

The flashing dot drew closer. Now on the main road. It zeroed in on them. Does it know their location? "It's heard him and his stupid shouting."

Her right hand ached. "But she can't let up. Slow down now and they'd be screwed. If only he knew what would happen. He'd keep his mouth shut then. Maybe Joni should shut it for him? Did she have time?" She leaned right, whipping the bike into a tight turn. The right wheels lifted from the ground. She forced her weight over them, and the board slammed down. *Crash!* But the trailer slid out behind.

Crack!

The trailer flipped. The turn too sharp.

Crack!

Crack!

Crack!

It turned over and over. Plastic hitting concrete. Joni let go of the throttle. The trailer turned three more times and slammed into the wall. Wheels faced the grey sky. They still turned. His shouting had stopped.

The dot on her scanner closed in. "It's already heard us.

Him. It's already heard him. Him and his stupid shouting. Stupid boy. The game's up for Joni because of him." She unclipped her scanner. She left her board. The strap attached to the trailer had twisted. "How many flips? Five? Six?" The dot drew closer.

Joni lifted the plastic trolley, but halted. They appeared on her right. They'd come from one of the many roads. Like rats in the sewers, they could come from anywhere. They smelled weakness. Dirty faces, they held clubs, bats, and crude knives. Rusting steel and bent blades. Those kinds of cuts were much harder to heal. One to two hundred of them. That many and they were still quieter than him. Her noisy passenger. Not so noisy now. Bit late to take a vow of silence.

Joni grunted with the effort of pulling the trolley. She dragged it up onto its side and let it fall onto its wheels. It slammed down. The two passengers lay still. Eyes closed. Dead?

Two fingers along the side of his neck. The one with the bandages. Fresh bloodstains leaked through. A pulse. Weak, but he still had a pulse. But for how much longer?

The dot closed in. The dirty army stepped towards them.

The noisy one's pulse beat harder. Were he conscious, he'd still be shouting.

Joni pulled the button from her bag. She held it in her left hand, her scanner in her right. The people halted. Of course they did. They knew what this meant. Game over. Only one winner, no matter how they stacked the odds. Two hundred to one or two thousand to one. Several hissed until she held up the scanner for them to see. The flashing dot closed in on them like it closed in on her. If it arrived, all of them were screwed. It had left the main road. It followed Joni's path.

The army bared their teeth. The bright glow of enamel against dirty skin. A low growl of hostility. They fixed on her. They tightened their grips on their weapons. Their jagged and crude weapons. But they'd still cut a throat. Just not today.

Back on her wheeled board. She reattached the scanner to the handlebars. It continued to give her a flashing warning of how little time remained. A slight turn of the throttle. The board rolled forwards. The strap pulled taut. The trailer moved with her. It moved just fine. The only damage from the crash had happened to the shouting man.

The button in her hand. If the army didn't move to let her pass, she'd damn well make them. Only one winner. The language barrier didn't matter. They understood one another. They moved aside. Gave her a clear path through. Some swayed while watching her. Some raised their clubs. Some stepped closer, their faces twisted.

The dot halted. Joni's heart beat in her throat. They didn't need to know. She turned the throttle and sped up. She waved the button at anyone too close. They stepped back. Didn't need to be told twice.

The dot hovered halfway between her and the main road. Maybe it hadn't heard them. And it wouldn't hear them now. Unconscious. Both of them. She should have thrown him into the wall sooner.

Another twist of her throttle. Half the people pressed against the walls. The other half retreated down the tight alley they'd come from. Tails between their legs. Weapons lowered. "No one crosses Joni. They know what they get."

The static dot at her back. The people pulling away. The button out ahead of her to make sure they stayed where they were. And two quiet passengers. Get through this and she'd be home free. "Joni told him to be quiet. Joni told him what would happen if he didn't. But he didn't listen. This is what happens to those who don't listen. You get what you deserve."

The last of the army retreated. The way clear, Joni took

off. The strap attaching the trailer to her wheeled board whipped against the insides of her legs.

"Maybe next time you'll listen to Joni." She said it too quietly for him to hear. Not that he could hear her, anyway. "Joni knows best. Nothing can stop her. The sooner you learn that, the easier this will be for you."

CHAPTER 2

Gracie ran next to Matilda, matching her stride for stride. Nothing would stop her, and Gracie understood. Never one to make a fuss or take charge, Matilda usually held back. The embodiment of quiet confidence. She did everything well. She could run for days. She could fight with the best of them. She could climb anything. The perfect person to have in a group. Her ego didn't get in the way, and her actions were always just. She'd voice an opinion when needed, and she didn't take charge for the sake of it. But right now, she led, and they followed. They were heading after the woman who'd taken Artan and Nick.

A grey concrete on the ground. Gunmetal grey steel flanking them. Sentry guns ran along the tops of the walls like those they'd avoided when they'd climbed into the place. Hopefully, the guns only activated when they sensed someone up high. They didn't stand a chance if they turned on them while they were on the ground. Paths led from the main road on either side of them. They forked and branched, plunging deeper into this maze of a place. But they weren't planning on following any of them. Instead, they fixed on the gigantic building miles away in the distance. The mountainous construction where the guards had gone. The direction the lady had taken Artan and Nick until she'd turned off.

"Oh, shit!" Gracie slowed her pace with heavy slamming steps. Fatigue ran through her veins like tar. She'd told herself, when they were climbing the wall, that she'd rest on the other side. Fat chance! The others slowed around her. Even Matilda.

Hawk's face glistened with sweat. He gulped, bringing Gracie's attention to the dryness in her own throat. "You think it's seen us?"

Gracie shook her head. The small, dark grey quadruped stood about a mile away. "Not yet. Come on." She ran right onto one of the narrower roads. About a third of the size of the main road, it stretched about fifteen feet wide. The walls stood as tall. Fifty feet, they loomed large, leaning over the group, reminding them how small they were by comparison.

Matilda overtook Gracie and set the pace, leading them on. Diversion or not, they were still on Artan and Nick's trail.

The path followed the same pattern as the main road. Branches led away from it on either side. More like alleys than roads, they invited them to travel deeper into the labyrinthine sprawl they'd seen when they overlooked this place. Matilda passed several turns before she took a left and slowed to a walk.

They crossed a white line about three feet thick. It ran across the road and up the walls on either side. Hawk's mouth hung open, his Adam's apple prominent when he looked up. Glass domes sat directly on top of the white paint. "What are all these lines about?"

"And what do the lights mean?" Olga said. "Are they always off? What happens if they come on?"

William scratched his head. "Part of me wonders if it's best we never find out."

Matilda stopped around the next bend. "Shit!" The road split into three. "It was easier on the main road. We had something to head towards and a clear line of sight."

"But we're less exposed in these tighter paths," Gracie said.

"I just hope Artan and Nick are okay," Matilda said.

"Of course." Gracie filled her lungs, her hands on her hips. Three paths. Which one should they take? Matilda's face a mess of worry lines, Gracie said, "We'll do all we can to get to them."

William took Matilda's hands in his. "I promise you we'll find them before anything happens."

Matilda's frown deepened, and she dropped her head.

"I'd die for you and Artan," William said. "You know that, right?" He shook her hands when he said it again. "Right?"

Matilda replied to the ground. "Right."

"If it's the last thing I do, I'll make sure we find them before anything happens. I promise."

Not a promise Gracie would have made. Who knew what they'd come across in a place like this? Who knew if anyone of them would get out alive.

"But something's already happened," Matilda said. "That woman's taken them."

"Artan's a fighter. He'll keep himself and Nick safe until we get to them. They'll be okay."

"We're all here for you, Matilda." Gracie rested a hand on her back. "Artan and Nick are a part of this group. We'll do everything in our power to find them. The best we can do right now is keep heading in this direction. We'll get to the guards' building soon enough. That's where we'll find our answers."

"But which path do we take?" Matilda said. "One of these three has to be the best option. Which one is it?"

Hawk hung back with Olga. He leaned out of the end of the alley, looking back the way they'd come from. Gracie raised her eyebrows at him, and he shook his head. The dog hadn't followed them.

A painted white line about ten feet into each alley. A line to cross. But to cross into what? What did they even mean? What were they triggering by walking over them?

William drew his sword. "Wait here and watch our backs."

Matilda shook her head, her brow locked in a frown. "Where are you going?"

William pointed with his sword down the pathway on their right. "To check out what's going on down this one. We should at least do a cursory check of each option before making a choice. It might give us something."

Olga drew her sword next and ran after William. "I'll go with you."

"We can't just stand here waiting." Matilda nodded at the central alley. "I'll check this one."

"I'm coming too," Hawk said.

Gracie raised her hand. "Wait!"

Matilda turned her palms to the sky. "For what?"

"One of us should watch our backs."

"But the dogs aren't coming," Hawk said.

"I still think one of us needs to stay here. I'll do it. If we get company, I'll let you know."

Already turning away from her, Matilda said, "Okay."

Both sets of friends vanished from sight, leaving Gracie on her own. How far would they go before they came back? How long should she wait before she got concerned? Should she have established that before they left?

Gracie returned to the street they'd taken from the main road. She leaned against the cold steel wall, the brushed surface rough against her shoulder. She peered back the way they'd come. Back towards the main road. She kept most of her body hidden. If she needed to vanish in a hurry, she could. There was still no dog. There's no way it would have seen them from the distance. Good job they'd seen it first. Her experience with the nasty things had stood her in good stead. They'd been a part of her world for so long, she'd developed a hypersensitivity to them. They represented just one thing to her: Death. Too many people had left Dout and never returned. Too many people had been burned alive … she shuddered. Too many people.

Clack-clack!

A dog burst from a smaller path on Gracie's left. About one hundred feet away. She pulled back into the alley and leaned against the wall. She rode out her quickened breaths, her heart pounding.

Clack-clack!

Another one joined the first. But they hadn't seen her. Look again and they almost definitely would.

Slow and deliberate steps, Gracie backed away from the wider road. Closer to the fork. Three choices. She had to decide on one. She said she'd let them know if there were any problems. But how could she let them know? Shout and she'd definitely give away their location. Maybe the dogs would go the other wa—

Clack-clack!

Clack-clack!

"Shit!" Several more dogs joined the pack.

Clack-clack!

Clack-clack!

Steel feet against concrete.

They were heading straight for her.

Gracie wrapped a fist around her mum and dad's

wedding rings. The metal dug into her palm. She had to make a choice.

Clack-clack!

Clack-clack!

She ran down the middle path after Hawk and Matilda.

Clack-clack!

She crashed into Hawk's back. He spun on her with his knife raised. He tilted his head to one side. "What are you doing here?"

"Keep your voice down."

Matilda peered around Gracie as if she could see past the bend in the path. "What's happened?"

"Dogs." Gracie's cheeks puffed with her exhale. "They came from another direction."

"They saw you?"

"They would have had I not run."

"And what about Olga and William?"

"I'm sorry, Matilda. I had to choose one path. I could only warn one of you. If I'd have shouted, they would have heard m—"

"Why choose us?"

"Because they have swords."

Matilda shrugged.

"And they have Olga. She's a one-woman army."

Tears glazed Matilda's eyes, and her cheeks flushed red. She nodded, her lips tight while she breathed in through her nose. "You're a good person, Gracie. You make selfless choices. You always have the best of intentions. That's all that matters. It was an impossible decision."

Hawk turned his palms to the sky. "So what do we do now?"

Clack-clack!

Clack-clack!

Gracie bounced on the spot. "They've split up. They're

coming down all three paths. We have to keep moving. We have to head to the building where the guards went."

"You think William and Olga will go that way?"

"Yes. Once they lose the dogs. What else can they do?"

Clack-clack!

Clack-clack!

"Come on." Hawk took off.

Gracie nodded at Matilda, who nodded back. They followed Hawk away from the dogs, and away from their friends.

CHAPTER 3

"You think this will take us to that massive building?"

William squinted. The sun had broken through the clouds and shimmered off their brushed-steel surroundings. The path curved away from them to the right, giving them a view of about one hundred feet both ahead and behind. "I think all roads lead to that place eventually, and seeing as we've not seen any issues ahead."

"We've not seen much of anything ahead," Olga said.

"But we can't see any issues."

"If you close your eyes in a room filled with diseased …"

"I get your point, but this is hardly a room filled with diseased. And, unless we're on the main road, we won't have a good view on which to base our decisions. The walls are too tall."

"If you're happy to tell the others the way's clear, then I'll go with it."

"I'm happy to tell them we couldn't see very far, and if we had to make a choice, this seems as good a choice as any." William glanced back. "We've already been away from them for longer than I'd like. I shouldn't have left Matilda. That was a stupid idea. We could have checked out the paths one at a time and gone as a group. I was too keen to be the hero."

"Maybe it's worked in our favour." Olga shrugged. "Maybe they've found a better route than this. Maybe we would have settled for this one when there are preferable options out there."

"Or maybe they've run into trouble. We need to get back." William pointed his sword the way they'd come. He paused for a second to give Olga the chance to reply. When she didn't, he led them away.

Because they'd turned around, the sloping bend in the path now leaned to the left. They crossed the same white line they'd passed over on their way down the tunnel. The thick glass domes covering the lights sat atop the walls on either side. What would it mean if they came on? The sun might have broken through the clouds, but the grey floor and tall steel walls clung to the cold, keeping their environment chilled. Adrenaline flooded William's system. He clamped his jaw, his body locked tight. No matter how light his steps, the narrow path and tall walls threw his progress back at him. Threw it back at him, back at anyone else listening, and ahead, should there be anyone around the corner who wanted to know they were coming. They—

A sharp pain bit into William's right arm. Olga yanked him back.

William kept his voice low and spoke through gritted teeth. "What?"

Olga raised the index finger on her right hand and tilted her ear towards the sky to encourage him to listen.

They didn't have time for this. They needed to get back to Matilda and the others. William tugged against her grip, but she held on, her fingers stinging the inside of his bicep. "What is it, Olga? Just tell me. Wh—"

Clack-clack!

Clack-clack!

"Shit!"

Olga raised her eyebrows.

"What do we do?"

"What can we do? We turn around."

"No." William shook his head. He pulled against Olga's grip again. "We need to get back to Matilda and the others."

"We'll get cremated long before we reach them."

"So Matilda's no longer a priority?"

"Surely our number one priority has to be survival?"

"And give up on Matilda and the others?"

"This is the opposite of giving up, William."

"Doesn't sound like it."

Clack-clack!

"The only thing around that bend is death."

Clack-clack!

Clack-clack!

The weight of his sword in his right hand, William tugged against Olga again, and this time she let go.

"I get what you're saying, William. I really do, but right now, we have a binary choice. We either die or we run. You and I both know getting back to Matilda in this moment isn't an option. We need to save ourselves first so we're alive to save them later."

Clack-clack!

"We know what those dogs can do. There's no situation where we come out on top in a fight against them."

Clack-clack! Clack-clack!

Multiple dogs. William's heart pulled him towards them. But he followed Olga, breaking into a jog. They ran back across the white line. Away from the dogs and away from Matilda and the others. Olga had a point. He'd made a promise to Matilda. A promise he couldn't honour if he got barbecued by a pack of robotic canines.

CHAPTER 4

"Nice and tight. Joni will make sure you're tied nice and tight. She doesn't want you rolling away now, does she? Sorry if she's a bit rough, but she has to be quick. Your friend is in danger up there. Someone might find him if she's too slow. And you'll be okay once Joni ties you in. You won't have any problems down here. Are you okay, dear?" Not that he heard her. The bandaged young man had been cut to shreds and beaten. They'd knocked him unconscious, and that was how he'd stayed. "And Joni didn't help when she flung you both into the wall. But she needed to get away. We didn't have time. And your friend is awfully noisy. So Joni will tie you up and get him. She needs to make sure that when you wake up, you don't panic and roll away. Panicking won't get you anywhere." She pulled on the straps again, smiled, and stepped back. "You're nice and tight. Just right. Fight or flight. Do as you might." Three straps across him. One ran across his chest, one across his stomach, and one over his legs. Each one pinned him in place. Held him to the bed. She felt the back of his neck again. "Nice and tight and scar-free. No one will find you here. Joni will take care of you."

Joni ran from the room and shoved the door closed. A little too hard, it slammed shut.

Crash!

Her shoulders snapped to her neck. Her heart pounded. "Keep the noise down, will ya? Someone will hear." She locked the door.

Thunk!

The sound echoed in her small home, the main living space now filled with what she'd kept in her storage room. Not a storage room anymore. The guest bedroom. And she couldn't put her things in the oubliette. That was for him. For the day she got him down here to be forgotten about. It needed to remain empty. Ready for the moment the opportunity arose. One day, he'd be hers. One day, the tables would turn.

The screens flickered. Twenty different images. Twenty different viewpoints. Ever changing, but playing the same dreary narrative of this place. "All of them but one. One never moved. Until today." It still pointed in the wrong direction. Knocked aside by one of the climbers. She held her chin in a pinch. "Who moved it? Not him in there. No. He couldn't do anything in that state. How did he even get over the wall? The other one? Did he kick it? The shouter? The noisy one. Until Joni silenced him. He needed it. She'd do it again. But what if he doesn't wake up? Surely his fault. Shouldn't have shouted so much. Like he wanted to give them away. Like he wanted to be found. But this isn't the kind of place you want to be found in. Oh no. He'll thank Joni at some point. They all will." Joni knocked her own head with her fist. "Joni needs to be quick. No time to mess around. Stop getting distracted."

Joni gathered up the length of rope and slid the metal peg

into her back pocket. She had no time. She had to be quick. Exposed up there on his own. If anyone found him, it would be game over for all of them. After all these years. A rookie error. "No." She shook her head. "Not today, thank you. Not today."

Joni returned to the ladders, her wheeled board and trailer against the wall. Her arms shook with fatigue. She trained hard and kept herself fit. She could carry the bandaged boy down here on the trailer, but she couldn't get them both down at once. "She has to hurry. Out there, he's exposed. We're all exposed."

The rungs embedded in the wall were rough with rust. She climbed back up to the hole, the rope slung over one shoulder and across her front. Before she climbed out of reach, she grabbed the trolley and focused on her exit again. The bright sky stung her sore eyes. "Joni's already had a long day. She'll sleep well tonight. Like a baby. Like the dead."

At the top of the ladder, Joni crawled out of the hole, the prickly ridges of rough concrete sore against her knees. Like thorns in the ground. Like tiny frozen waves. She dragged the trolley up behind her and laid it next to him. Straps on the trolley, similar to the ones she'd used to keep his friend in the bed. She'd taken too much time with his friend. She'd left him up here on his own for too long. What if he came to now?

Joni ran her fingertips over the back of the boy's neck. "Neither of them are scarred. They really did come from the other side of the wall. But why? Who'd choose to come here?" She rolled the unconscious boy into the trolley and tightened the straps. Her hands shook with her haste. She tied the rope in a knot around the front of his wheeled stretcher. "Joni will keep you safe from harm. She has your best interests at heart. Joni is here to protect you. Few people can say that. Not much protection in a place like this.

Exploitation, yes. Death, certainly. Not much protection. Joni is a protector. Joni's the best person for you to be with right now."

Pushing her foot against the front of the trolley, Joni pulled with her whole body. A tug of war to test the knot. "Nice and tight now." She tugged again. "Nice and tight. The knot will hold."

A check around. Joni sniffed the air. She'd left her tracker on her wheeled board's handlebars. "A rookie error! Joni should know better than that." The nearby building's vast shadow spilled across her and her surroundings like black ink. An alley on her right on the other side of the tall wall. She lived in a spot rarely visited. "But not never. No, not never. Don't get complacent, Joni. They visit everywhere eventually." She rapped her knuckles against the side of her head. "Joni needs to get on with it. She needs to be quick."

Half-crawling, half-running, Joni moved like a primate. The peg in her back pocket was about six inches long and an inch wide. She wedged it into the gap she'd made years previously and stamped on it. "Joni has done this before. With things heavier than that boy. Don't panic, Joni. Everything will be fine. You can do this." From her crouched position, she peered up at the tall building. She cowered in the face of its looming authority. It wouldn't always be an authority. She'd get to him one of these days. She'd take it all away. Burn it to the ground. "Come on, Joni!" She needed to hurry. She wiggled the peg. "Snug, bug, pug. Peg, beg, in the bed." She looped the rope around it and ran back to the entrance to her home and the boy on the trolley.

The rope wrapped around her waist, Joni eased the trolley closer to the hole. It teetered on the edge for a second before it fell. The rope snapped taut, yanking her back towards the peg. She planted her feet, grunting as she halted her slide. He hung down into her home. Strapped to the trolly, suspended in mid-air.

"One small step at a time." Joni stepped towards the peg, letting the rope out, lowering the trailer little by little. "Joni can do this a small step at a ti—"

The whirring stopped her dead. Her heart kicked, forcing the breath from her lungs. "Huh?"

The wind dragged Joni's hair across her face. Her ragged pulse throbbed through her ears. "No." She shook her head and smiled. "It's nothing. There's nothing comi—"

The whirring drew closer. A drone!

"Joni's a stupid idiot. She left her device in her home. She could have seen them coming. Could have done something about it. Could have planned. Best laid. Now wasted. Her device could have told her everything. What's wrong with her? A rookie. All these years and she's behaving like a rookie."

The alley's tight walls amplified the drone's hum.

Steps towards the peg, the trailer dropping into her home. Joni tried to stop at three, but the weight of the boy on the trailer pulled her forwards two more steps. The soles of her boots slid over the rough concrete. The small waves. The thorny spikes.

Joni leaned back against the boy and the trolley's weight. She rode her ragged breaths. The peg just a few feet away.

The drone drew closer.

The peg now at the end of her reach. She pulled it from the ground. A cork from a bottle.

Thwip!

The rope snapped taut again, spinning Joni around and dragging her back to the hole.

The peg in her right hand, she held the rope with her left. Her arm shook, holding the weight of the boy on the trailer. Sweat dampened her brow. The thick rope chewed into her palm. The hum grew louder. Joni wound her right arm back, the hand holding the peg.

"One try. Make it count."

On the edge of her balance, she leaned against the boy's weight. Joni's arm shook. Her left hand burned. The drone's hum, a large wasp closing in. Joni threw the steel peg.

It sailed through the air in a wide arc. It spun as it flew. Light enough to launch. Heavy enough to make a sound.

Clang!

It hit the top of the wall closest to her. Joni winced. It fell over the other side.

Clang!

It hit the concrete in the unseen alley.

The humming quietened. The drone had stopped. Had Joni done enough? She stilled, save for her trembling form. She held the boy and the trolley, her left shoulder aching. Drop him now and the drone would hear. All over. After all this time. A rookie error. Her scanner in her home.

The drone flew away. It had gone to investigate. Joni relaxed with a hard exhale. "But Joni must hurry. The drone won't be long. When they find the peg, they will come to investigate. There can't be any sign of Joni when that happens."

Trembling with every step, Joni gripped the rope with both hands. She found her footing, held the boy's weight, and stepped forward again.

The rope slackened. He'd reached the ground. Joni let go, slipped into the hole, and climbed down several rough rungs before she pulled the large steel disc covering her home over the top. It slotted into place with a *clunk!*

Joni's hard exhale echoed in her small home. "She's made it. She's beaten them again. Joni always wins. He knows it. They all know it."

At the bottom of the ladder, the boy and the trailer lay

face down. Joni flipped them back over. “Welcome to Hell’s waiting room.” She laughed and rolled the boy to the guest bedroom. The boy with the bandages had stolen her bed, and now this one had taken the space where she stored her supplies. All the things she’d taken from him. She now had to keep them in her living space. “The discomfort one endures to ensure their guests have a pleasant stay!”

The straps would hold him in place like they held his friend. “Nice and tight. No chance of him getting out until Joni decides. For their own good. Joni knows best.”

Joni locked the door.

Thunk!

Filled with the warmth of her grin, she’d not grinned like this in such a long time. Joni stared at the rusty steel door. They were safe for now.

CHAPTER 5

Every one of Gracie's steps sent a slamming jolt through her as she fought to keep pace with Matilda and Hawk. Fought to keep pace with her friends and fought her own exhaustion. They'd been on the run for hours. The air had cooled as they moved deep into the afternoon. The sky chocked with clouds, the tall walls emitted a chill befitting their stark, gunmetal grey appearance.

No matter how many times they'd turned left or right, they ran down the same bland alley. The same tall walls. The same grey ground. The occasional white line cut across their path, but how could they call that only real change in their stark surroundings progress? But at least they'd made it over the wall. And at least they'd evaded the dogs. They knew little about this place, but they knew the capability of the small beasts. Come head-to-head with those things and there would only be one winner.

"You know," Gracie said, her words thrown back at her with her heavy steps, "were Olga on her own, I still might have come with you. Even alone, I think she'd handle herself better than the rest of us."

Thick bags beneath Matilda's brown eyes. Her dark skin shone with a layer of sweat. She maintained her pace, her face tight, her roving attention scanning their monotonous environment. Surely she'd find some small sign where the others were. "I hope you're right. I hope we see them again soon."

"We will." Hawk flicked his head to the right. "And we'll find Artan and Nick. Then we can get out of here. We just need to get to that massive building. They'll be there. I wouldn't mind betting they'll get there before us. Hopefully, they'll find the others while they're waiting."

"You don't think they'll do something different?" Matilda said. "I know we'd planned to meet there, but what if they change their mind? What if they're spending their time trying to find us?"

"They won't be." Hawk shook his head. "It makes little sense. We've already said where we'll meet. To deviate from the plan will only cause problems. As much as we all want to be back together, they'll see reason."

The soles of Gracie's boots scraped the rough concrete, her heavy steps clumsy with fatigue. The tall walls on either side probably stood dead straight, but from this close, they appeared to lean over them. "So how do we get to the guards' building? It feels like we're running in circles."

"The sun," Hawk said. Like Matilda, he had thick black bags beneath his bloodshot eyes. He stared up at the cloudy sky, stretching his scarred neck, the livid crimson marks from both the lashings and where the rope had bitten into his skin. Action and reaction. "It rises in the east and sets in the west. If we're heading south, we want it to rise on our left and set on our right."

"You've been following that all along?" Gracie said.

"I thought that's what we've all been doing?"

"So we've been heading in the right direction?"

"Yeah."

"And there's me thinking we're winging it."

Matilda raised her eyebrows. "It's a good job one of us is on the ball."

For most of the run, Gracie had only seen about one hundred feet ahead before the road curved away from sight. A never-ending path to nowhere. But the sun hung over to their right. They were on a never-ending path heading south.

Hawk continued leading them. He turned left and right before he gasped and stopped. The infinite path opened up into something more. A wider space. A vast roof that stood about five feet from the ground. "What is this place?" Gracie said.

Matilda walked towards it. "It looks like some kind of arena or hall. They've built it into the ground."

The rectangular roof stretched several hundred feet wide and about half that distance deep. Made from the same gunmetal grey steel as everything else, but thinner than the walls and gates, and crimped to form corrugated waves.

Gracie jogged to catch up with Matilda. She reached the roof at the same time as her. Cold to touch, windows filled the five-foot gap between the ground and the roof. The wall of glass flooded the underground arena with natural light.

Gracie crouched, Matilda on her left and Hawk on her right. She cupped her face with both hands to shut out what little glare came from the cloudy sky. The glass as cold as the roof, she leaned against it with the sides of each hand.

They'd seen places similar to this before. The words caught in Gracie's throat. She coughed to clear it and forced them out. "It reminds me of the sporting arena in Dout."

"Or the stadium in the ruined city," Hawk said. "Smaller, but I reckon you could still fit a few thousand people inside."

Matilda remained pressed against the window, her words deadened from where she spoke directly to the glass. "We had something similar in the national service area in Edin. They made us compete in a series of games in front of a crowd. As if national service wasn't hard enough."

"What do you think they do here?" Hawk said.

Gracie sat cross-legged on the rough concrete. "Some kind of sport." A red circle in the centre, a black plus sign within that circle. "Who knows?"

"Maybe we should ask them," Hawk said.

Gracie leaned towards the window again and cupped her face. She squinted into the darkness. The place stood empty. "Ask who?"

"Them."

The single syllable dropped a cold, dead weight of dread through Gracie's stomach. Hawk had pulled away from the window and turned to their left.

"Shit!" Matilda said.

Men and women with a scattering of children. About one hundred in total. Many of them carried clubs and batons. Crude weapons. The weapons of savages.

Matilda took off in the other direction. Gracie and Hawk followed.

The crowd gave chase. They yelled in a language Gracie recognised from the fights Dout had been dragged into over the years. Fights that plunged the depths of savagery and sadism. It was what these people brought to a battle. They were the scum of the earth.

The arena on their left, the crowd behind them. Matilda headed down one of the many pathways leading away from there.

Hawk shook his head. "I knew we shouldn't have come here."

The sun on their right. Even in their escape, Matilda led them towards the enormous building the guards had headed for.

Back on the tight roads, flanked by the vast walls. The pack behind drowned out their echoing steps.

"We can outrun them," Gracie said.

Matilda took the next left.

A roar on their right. Gracie jumped. Another thirty to forty savages had joined the chase.

The path split again. Matilda turned right, but spun back a second later. Their route cut off. More people. She chose the left path.

"There are too many of them," Hawk said. "I knew we shouldn't have come here."

Gracie didn't have the breath to reply, and Matilda seemed too preoccupied with picking a route. They were one wrong choice away from a brutal death. Complaining wouldn't get them anywhere.

The next road ran straighter than most. Another white line about one hundred feet ahead. The glass domes covered lights on the tops of the walls on either side. Whatever the lines meant, it represented a destination. Cross it and something would change. But what?

Another crowd of people appeared. About twenty strong. They blocked the road and their access to the white line. Matilda slowed. Many of the people were red faced from their run. Many were armed. The mob closed in from behind. No matter where Gracie and her friends went, these people would find them. They owned this maze.

Gracie halted beside Matilda. "We're screwed. I know these people. They have no mercy or compassion. Not for people like us." A crowd two to three hundred strong behind them. The crowd in front too dense to pass. Even if they got through, they couldn't outrun them all.

Hawk gasped for breath. His words fell from him. "What do we do?"

The caterwauling siren on the gates sounded. It snapped

through the group ahead of them, many of them staring in the noise's direction. The whine soared through the tight roads, flooding the place with its wailing cry. "They're opening the gates again so soon?" Gracie said.

The siren continued in the distance, but the people returned their attention to Gracie and her friends.

Matilda threw down her sword. It hit the rough concrete with a *clang!* She raised her hands above her head and spoke from the side of her mouth. "You might be wrong about these people. They would have already attacked by now if they wanted us dead."

"I'm not wrong"—Gracie threw down her knife—"but what can we do? It'll be much worse if we don't comply. Either way, we're screwed." She pressed her right palm to her chest, the lump of her mum and dad's wedding rings against her hand. She raised her arms in surrender. "If we try to fight them now, there will only be one winner."

"Shit!" Hawk's voice bounced off the walls. He still clung to his knife. Those ahead of them snapped tense. Grips tightened on weapons. They needed his compliance.

Hawk threw down his knife. His broad chest rose and fell with his ragged breaths. He too raised his hands above his head. "I can't help feeling that if we'd gotten across that line, we'd be home free."

"Think about it all you like," Matilda said. "We didn't make it."

"No." Hawk shook his head and spoke to the ground. "No, we didn't."

CHAPTER 6

William lost his breath when Olga slammed into him. Tackling him across the chest, she dragged him into an alley and slammed him against the wall.

"What the f—"

Olga pressed her finger to her lips. She lifted her left ear to the sky. He needed to listen.

His back against the cold steel wall, William shrugged. "What? What ca—"

Olga pressed her finger to her lips again. Harder than before.

Ringing steel. The tone both distant and consistent. It sang with a high-pitched metallic hum. Something hurtled towards them. Not the buzzing monotony of a drone, or the clacking of a galloping dog. William caught himself before he spoke for a third time. Olga clearly had better hearing than him.

The ringing grew louder, amplified by the acoustics of the tall walls. Whatever closed in on them moved fast. William gripped his sword's handle.

Whoom!

It flew past the end of the alley, disturbing the air, dragging on William's clothes.

"What th—"

Whoom!

A second vehicle shot past. Both of them were huge compared to the dogs and drones. The ringing steel quietened as they got farther away.

"I'm guessing they weren't searching for us, then," Olga said.

"No. They were heading somewhere with purpose." William poked his head from the end of the alley. The two vehicles were identical. Two eight-foot-tall circles, both of them about four feet wide. They had seats suspended on a static inner circular ring, a guard in each. The outside comprised two parallel chain tracks. Each track about six inches thick. They should have chewed into the concrete, but they left no trace, the call of their momentum the only evidence of their passing.

The lead vehicle leaned into the upcoming bend and vanished from sight. The one behind disappeared a few seconds later, and the hum of their momentum faded to nothing.

Olga had also leaned from the alley's entrance. Shorter than William, she stood in front of him but kept his line of sight clear. She whistled. "That was close."

"Too close."

"We need to give this up."

"Give up on Matilda? We could have run into those vehicles anywhere."

"But we didn't, did we? We ran into them here. And if we head towards the building like we all agreed when we were up on the wall, we wouldn't be here." Olga pointed from the alley at the wall on the other side of the road. Another sentry gun on the top, like the one they'd seen tear a bird to shreds.

They were everywhere. "That's the cross I scratched into the wall."

William dropped his attention to where Olga pointed. The shine of a freshly scored cross on an already heavily scratched surface.

"This is the *third* time we've passed it. We're walking in circles. How's that helping anyone?"

William slumped against the wall.

"Look." Olga grabbed his hands. "I get it, I really do, but the one thing both of our groups know is that we agreed to head to that massive building we saw the guards going towards. That place is our best hope of finding Artan, and I guarantee you Matilda and the others are on their way there."

"You can't guarantee me anything."

"Okay, you're right. But it's an educated guess, which is the best we have right now."

"Let's say we decide to head to that building." William threw up his arms and let them fall against his sides with a slap. "How do we know what way it is?"

"The sun rises in the east and sets in the west."

"Don't patronise me, Olga."

"I'm not. And it's okay if you didn't think about it. We've had to deal with a lot. But, if we're heading south, towards the tower, the sun will rise on our left and set on our right."

"But what if she's close? What if she's in trouble?"

"We're *all* in trouble. This entire place is trouble. And she might be close, but she could also be miles away."

"I've known Matilda a long time."

"I know."

"We grew up together. We spent as much time as we could together. Once, when I was about eight years old, I was eating dinner with my mum and dad. Something told me I had to go to Matilda's house. I put down my cutlery and ran.

Both Mum and Dad shouted at me, but I knew I couldn't stay. I'd never run to her house so fast. I knocked on her door, and her dad answered. Red faced and sweating, he had his belt in his hand. It had a thick steel buckle that was larger than my small fists. His eyes"—William shuddered, and his stomach tightened—"they were black. I know it sounds crazy, but he wasn't human in that moment. But then the blackness left his glare. Several people on the street had seen him. They must have held a mirror up to him. Shown him he'd gone too far. And sure, he went back in and gave Matilda a beating like he'd done many times before. But he always stopped. Matilda said, for the first time in her life, she didn't think he'd stop. That if I hadn't interrupted him, she would have died."

"What are you saying?"

"Something's wrong." William pressed his hand to his heart. "I can feel it like I felt it on that day. She needs us."

"Were we at a loose end, I'd follow you. If we knew where they were, I'd follow you. But we're not, and we don't. What we know is they will try to get to that building."

William shook his head. "The second we give up our search is when we'll be the closest to finding them. If we persevere just that little bit longer ..."

"That's a very noble way of being. You'd die for her, and you won't give up on her. I get that. But this isn't about giving up, it's about letting go."

"What's the difference?"

"By letting go, you're trusting her to find her way to the meeting point. She's not that little girl at the mercy of her dad. That story only serves your current anxieties. I'm sure there are many times when her dad could have lost it completely and you weren't there to help. And she got through somehow. She's a strong young woman who has Hawk and Gracie with her. By letting go, we can get to the place they'll expect to find us. By letting go, you give us a better chance of survival. If we go to that building, we'll reach her sooner. We need to back ourselves to get there and let them do the same."

William rested the back of his head against the cold wall. He stared up at the cloudy sky and sent a hard sigh at the heavens. "Do you *really* think this is the right choice?"

"Honestly? I don't know. But it's the most logical, which makes it the best choice. Only time will tell us what the right choice is." Olga cupped her ear. "Hear that?"

William scowled as if compressing his forehead would somehow aid his hearing. The ring of steel in the distance. "More of those things?"

"Come on." Olga tugged on William's arm and led him deeper into the alley, the sun setting on their right.

The continuous ringing of the vehicles' momentum drew closer. Multiple vehicles. More than before. William quickened his pace. Maybe Olga had a point. They'd been walking in ever-increasing circles and not found Matilda and the others. They needed to try something else. But did that something else have to be heading towards the tower? He'd let Olga lead them for now, but could he really afford to ignore his instincts?

CHAPTER 7

"Two more mouths to feed now, Joni." Her voice echoed in the steel maintenance shaft. "Two strapping lads, and we all know strapping lads need plenty of calories to remain strapping. It's Joni's job to care for them now. Now she's taken them from him, she needs to show them what it means to belong. No"—she opened her hand so wide her fingers splayed, and she hit the side of her head with her palm—"not belong. What it means to be a guest in her home. What she saved them from. How bad things could have been had she not rescued them. She's their number one fan. They'll feel that and they'll be grateful."

Her knees were sore and her palms cold from where she crawled along the tight tunnel. The echo of her progress ran away from her. "Joni normally comes later. This place is still active right now. Still alive. It might be dark outside, but in here, they're all still awake. And she'd normally wait. Joni can go a day or two without food. She can bide her time. It's what she's been doing for years. But she can't expect the strapping lads to do the same. One of them needs to heal. And she needs to quieten the other one. He's been saying it again and again." She knocked on the side of her head, this time with a fist. "I'm hungry. I'm hungry. Again and again."

Riding her quickened heartbeat, she fought to control her breaths. "He's like a child. He always needs feeding. So what else can Joni do? She has to get his food. She can make him wait longer. Wait until there's a safe time to come here, but she has to shut him up. And who knows when he ate last? He's hungry. He needs feeding. There's only one way to fix that. Well ... two. But she's not like him. She tries to help, not destroy."

Her rucksack empty on her back, Joni passed over another grate. Another hallway, sterile like the rest of this place. Gunmetal grey corridors. Patrolling guards dressed from head to toe in grey uniforms. "Who's Joni kidding? She doesn't need to be worried about coming here. She can come whenever she likes. She owns this place. She has the run of it. The only thing that changes is where he goes. He's moved again, but she'll find him. She always finds him. And when she does ..." Joni grinned. "Oh, when she does."

The kitchens were empty. "As they should be." Many of them might still be awake, but there's no more food until tomorrow. The kitchen staff have gone home and won't be back until the morning. "That gives Joni the time she needs to take what she wants. To show these boys that Joni cares for them. That she can look after them. Give them a feast."

The grate looked directly down on one of the food prep tables. She slammed her palm against the edge. It swung into the kitchen, the hinges groaning with the motion. The blood ran to Joni's head, her pulse throbbing in her ears when she hung down into the kitchen. "Of course the place is empty. Joni said it would be. Joni's already checked. But better to be safe than sorry. Better to be sure."

Joni spun around in the shaft and exited feet first. She hung her legs down towards the table and slid out, landing with a *thud* on the steel surface. Dirty boots on the freshly cleaned prep area. She twisted her feet as she walked along it and dropped to the ground.

The same bleak gunmetal grey surroundings as everywhere else. Surfaces. Ovens. Hot plates … Brushed steel everywhere.

The place reeked of bleach from where they'd cleaned the kitchen. But the tang of the most recently cooked meal also hung in the air. Meat stew. Boiled vegetables. What they ate most nights. Joni ran to the fridge on tiptoes and pulled the heavy door wide. A chilled blast laid a prickled layer against her skin, lifting gooseflesh on her arms. "Joni might know this place and be able to move through it at this time of day, but he'd best be grateful when she comes home with his food. After all his moaning, if he doesn't say thanks …" She knocked her head again. Banish the thoughts. She had to look after them. She'd taken them both in. She wanted to care for them. Wanted to make sure he didn't get to them. She'd willingly taken this on. "But if he keeps telling her about his hunger …"

Joni dropped her bag in front of the fridge and filled it. "Don't let the darkness in, Joni. He's allowed to be hungry. We all need food." Carrots, peppers, cucumbers. She pulled out a chunk of cooked deer on a chilled steel plate. The meat they must have used in the stew. They needed their protein to keep them strong. Especially the injured one. Covered in cuts, he needed it more than most.

Voices outside snapped Joni rigid. Her heart in her throat and her bag now bulging. She pulled the zip across, closed it, and slung it over her shoulders. Heavy on her back, but not too heavy. "This isn't Joni's first rodeo. She knows how much she can carry and still be able to get out of here."

The voices continued outside. The steps closed in on the kitchen. Joni pulled a knife from the wall, liberating it from the magnetic strip. The blade about a foot long, the weak light caught its shining blade. "Let them find Joni. See who walks away from the encounter. No one ever lives to tell the tale. Let them come."

Joni crouched down behind a table.

The light in the room changed from where the guards filled the doorway.

She gripped the knife so hard her hand trembled.

But the guards moved on. Even with the grate hanging down.

"Joni doesn't need this awful thing." She replaced the knife. "Why use a knife, anyway? Knives are too obvious. And too quick."

A bottle of bleach on the floor. Joni lifted it, hopped up onto the steel table, and slid it into the maintenance shaft ahead of her.

"Wait!" one guard said from outside the room. They'd stopped walking.

Joni gasped. "No, Joni waits for no one." She slid her bag up after the bleach, gripped the edge of the shaft, and pulled herself into the steel tunnel. She turned in the shaft, leaned down, gripped the grate, pulled it towards her, and halted just before she clicked it shut.

The light changed again when the guards entered the room. "Why are we coming in here?" A man's voice. Deep, the words slow like he had trouble forming them. Like he didn't have the brain cells for so many consecutive syllables without stopping for breath.

"I thought I heard something."

"Heard what? There's *nothing* here."

Lying on her front, Joni's fingers ached from supporting the grate. An inch from clicking it shut. But she couldn't close it now. Not with them beneath. Her entire body shook. Sweat itched around her collar.

The two men's steps snapped around the kitchen. They walked in unison. Side by side.

"Come on, Frank," the stupid one said. "There's nothing here. Let's go."

Frank remained silent for several seconds before he finally said, "Fair enough."

The light changed again as the men left.

Click! Joni pulled the hatch shut. "Joni came here too early. She should know better. She came here because he complained about being hungry. Always complaining. They need to eat. Joni gets that. But they need to know when to ask for it. They need to not be such spoiled brats." She whacked her head with her knuckles. "He needs to learn. What can the other one do? With so many wounds, he might never wake up. But his friend. A spoiled little brat. He'd best appreciate what Joni's done for him. And if she hears about his hunger again, she'll cut his throat. Stab him in the eyes and cut his stupid throat."

~

AT HER CROSSROADS where all the tunnels met, the place where she'd stored her tinfoil tray, Joni stood in the vertical shaft and placed the bleach next to where she'd left the spanner to loosen the pipes. "This can go here for when Joni finds him. This will come in handy. She has more important things to do than look for him right now, but she can use this later. Why rush when she has a lifetime to destroy him?"

Tightening her backpack's straps, Joni rolled the bag so it lay evenly. She hunched down and crawled back towards her home, her jaw tight, her brow locked in a hard frown. "Joni has food for him, but so help him if he doesn't show her gratitude. So help him."

CHAPTER 8

Crack! Gracie's head snapped away from yet another blow. Her ears rang, and a coppery flow of blood ran down the back of her throat. But she held her footing and lifted her chin. She wouldn't give them what they wanted.

The boy in front of her couldn't have been any older than about fourteen. Skin and bones, he had a sharp and angular face, piercing blue eyes, and blond, floppy hair. His gaze flitted. He couldn't look her in the eyes. This clearly hadn't happened before. Why didn't she fight back?

White light flashed through Gracie's vision, and her legs wobbled. He'd caught her on the temple. Blood ran from her nose, over her lips, and dripped from her chin. She sniffed and straightened her back. She kept her hands by her sides.

They stood in a makeshift arena. A square plaza over one hundred feet wide and one hundred feet deep. The same concrete ground as everywhere else in this place. Cages ran around the square's perimeter, prisoners inside them. Hawk and Matilda were in one close by. Floodlights in each corner stood about twenty feet tall and shone on Gracie and the boy.

The spectators, both caged and uncaged, wouldn't miss a thing. The dark didn't stop them fighting here.

"Gracie! Fight back." Matilda pressed her face to her cage's bars. After they'd thrown down their knives, these savages had used them to force them to come here. They'd caged all three of them and singled out Gracie as the one to take a beating. Did they recognise her from Dout?

Gracie spat a globule of blood onto the concrete between her and her attacker. It shone in the floodlights. Many of the prisoners called and jeered from their cages. The people on the sidelines shouted louder. They all spoke a language Gracie didn't recognise. Even after all this time of being these people's enemy, she still didn't understand a word they said.

"Come on, Gracie." Hawk this time. He stood next to Matilda and held the bars in a tight grip like he might find the superhuman strength to force them wider. "Do something!"

"So they can torture—" *Crack!* Gracie stumbled when the boy struck her again. She wiped her bleeding mouth with the back of her sleeve and glared at him. She raised her voice for the benefit of the people on the sidelines. The uncaged agitators. "I won't let them win. This is what they do. They torture and goad people. They want me to fight back so they have an excuse to beat the life out of me. This is all a game to these savages. They're subhuman. They don't think like us."

The boy's face glistened with sweat. He swiped his floppy blond hair away from his forehead and bounced on his toes, his fists raised again. His brow furrowed when Gracie addressed him. He clearly didn't understand her either. "You need to give it up, son. I won't fight you."

He lowered his fists, but the people who'd brought him there, the ones outside the cages, shouted louder. He raised his guard again. He stepped forward, his features twisted.

Gracie kept her arms limp. Another white flash from yet another strike. Her head snapped to the side. Her nose ran with a fresh surge of blood. Her face throbbed.

A woman with wiry brown hair shoved through the spectators. She strode towards Gracie and the boy. Over six feet tall, she had biceps as thick as Gracie's waist. She walked with slamming steps, her shoulders pulled back. She leaned close, and Gracie ruffled her nose against the reek of her stale breath.

The blast of the woman's ferocity hit Gracie like a natural disaster. A storm of spittle. A hurricane of syllables. She had yellow teeth, cracked lips, and a crusty goatee of spots. Her greasy skin gave her face a glossy sheen.

Both Hawk and Matilda remained pressed up against the bars of their cage.

"I get you're pissed." Gracie shrugged. "But I don't understand a word you're saying."

The woman yelled again and poked Gracie hard in the chest.

Gracie stumbled back a step. She clamped her jaw and kept her arms at her sides. Don't give her the satisfaction.

Every subsequent poke harder than the one it succeeded. Each one added to the sting on her sternum. Gracie spoke through gritted teeth. "See what I mean? These people aren't human. I know these people. Dout has been fighting them for years." She stumbled back again from the force of the woman's shove. Although she spoke to her friends, she aimed her words at the woman. "The same people who take pleasure in torture and violence. It's a way of life for them."

"It's a way of life for all of us," Matilda said. "It's called survival."

"It's called sadism. There's a world of difference."

"You need to fight back."

"I won't lower myself to their standards." Gracie tripped

from the woman's next jab and landed on her arse. The shock of the impact ran up her spine, jarring every bone in her body.

Her face a crimson beacon, the hulking woman shoved her massive fists on her hips and leaned over Gracie. She screamed and yelled. She threw her hands out to the sides. She pointed back at the meek boy who'd spent the past few minutes punching her.

"She wants you to hit him back," Hawk said.

Gracie fought against the tension in her jaw and smiled up at the woman. The bottom half of her face soaked with her blood, a crimson spray burst from her when she said, "Of course she wants me to hit him back. Have you not been listening?"

"Maybe all they want is for him to have a fight," Matilda said. "A two-sided fight."

"Two-sided isn't a concept they understand, Matilda. They don't do fair. You don't know these people."

"Neither do you."

Gracie remained on her arse and turned to her friend, the sturdy woman still shouting at her. "I've met enough of them to know what they're like." She pointed up at the woman. "Evil's in their blood. I won't play their sick games."

Two men joined the woman. Both of them stood a few inches taller than her. Dressed in filthy rags, they had long matted hair and beards. They lifted Gracie beneath her armpits and forced her to stand. She went limp like a child so they had to support her weight.

They let go, and Gracie slammed into the concrete knees first. Rods of fire streaked up her thighs into her groin. Nausea balled in her stomach. If she bit down any harder, she'd drive her teeth back into her gums. But it helped her hold on to her scream. She shook her head. "Don't give them the satisfaction."

The men lifted Gracie again. Her knees still burned, but this time, she supported her own weight. The man on her right shoved her into the one on her left, who shoved her back. From one to the other, they toyed with her. Humiliated her.

Crack! The large woman slapped Gracie.

The left side of her face throbbing from the blow, Gracie's jaw ached, but she smiled anyway. "You slap harder than that boy punches."

The woman hit Gracie again. *Crack!* And again. *Crack!*

Gracie's ears rang, and her head spun. An adrenaline dump sent her pulse racing. The men's fingertips bit into the tops of her arms. The savage woman dragged the boy back towards her and barked a single word at him.

The boy shook his head and cried.

The same word. The woman barked it again.

His fists balled, the boy stared at the ground.

The woman leaned close to the boy and whispered in his ear. The words might have been lost on Gracie, but the hairs stood up on the back of her neck from where the low tone rolled with the ferocity of distant thunder.

His face a gurning, grieving mess, the boy stepped closer, raised a shaking fist, and punched Gracie again.

Fiery rods streaked down Gracie's back. The men's restraint made her body less able to absorb the blows. She sniffed against her running nose and fixed on the now-crying boy.

"The only way this ends for you," Matilda said, "is if you fight back."

"The end's coming no matter what I do." Gracie shook her head. "I refuse to give them the satisfaction of me retaliating. I won't justify this little boy's actions. He'll give up before I do."

"The others won't," Hawk said.

Everything Gracie had held onto flooded out. She shook with the force of her words. "You think I don't know that?" Her already watering eyes glazed further with a fresh surge of tears. "You think I didn't watch them take down Marcus through Dout's cameras? You think I didn't watch them goad him and shove him until he fought back?" She stamped her foot, her knees still sore. "You think I didn't watch them skin him alive when he retaliated? I know these people. I know what they're like."

"You don't."

Gracie turned to Matilda again. The boy punched her in the side of her head.

When Gracie lifted her chin, Matilda said, "You don't know this specific group of people. Don't be so sure you know where this is going."

The boy punched her again, and Gracie's legs wobbled. The men kept her standing. "Experience is all I have here, which is more than you. And experience tells me where this is going." The front of her top was now soaked with her blood. "I won't give them what they want." She turned to the boy. "I won't fight you!"

The men let go, and Gracie crumpled to the ground.

Her left eye swollen shut, Gracie winced when the boy pulled his leg back to kick her. She rested her hand against her chest. Her mum and dad's wedding rings pressed against her palm. But the boy paused. She might not have understood his language, but she understood his shaking head. She understood when he turned his back on her and walked away. She understood the fury in the large woman's taut frame. Even after the beating they'd just given her, even with her body throbbing from the attack, she smiled. "Whatever they plan on doing to me, I want no part in it. If they're going to kill me, let it expose them for the cowards they are."

CHAPTER 9

The spot where they'd seen the bikes now well behind them, William and Olga crossed another thick white line. Lights on the top of the walls on either side. Every time they passed one of these lines, William held his breath. Surely they existed for a reason? Although, what would he prefer, the anxiety about what could happen, or finding out what happened when the lights turned on?

William's gut urged him away from the guards' tower in search of Matilda and the others. But that instinct had no destination, so he followed Olga's lead. How could he take them deeper into this hellish labyrinth without knowing where they were heading? Olga had a logical plan. He didn't.

More sentry guns. Imposing mounds atop the walls, silhouettes against the night sky. They were everywhere. To the point where they almost became innocuous. Almost. He'd seen what they were capable of.

The sheer number of turnings and paths made William's head spin. Gunmetal grey walls loomed over them, the darkness of night deepening the shadows. The grey concrete ground stretched away. An easy place to lose yourself, but Olga kept them heading towards the tower. The sun had set on their right, and she'd somehow maintained their bearings. At least, she acted like she had. And how could he question it when he had nothing better to offer?

William quickened his pace, so he walked at Olga's side. "Thank you."

Some of the tension left her body, but she continued to scan their surroundings. "For what?"

"For what you did for us back at the wall when we were all hiding in the fog. I can't imagine it was easy leading that diseased horde away from us. Weren't you scared?"

Olga remained fixed ahead, so William only saw the right side of her face. The skin at the edge of her eye wrinkled, and she shrugged. "Not really."

"But you might have died."

"There are worse things that could happen."

Like losing someone you loved. William rubbed her back. She tensed and then relaxed a little, nodding at his gesture.

"So what happened while you were out there? Did you come close to not returning?"

"Ha!" Olga nodded again. "A few times, yeah. The fog helped, but there were a *lot* of them. Although, it was the hill at the end that nearly did me. I thought I was going to break my neck coming down that thing. I used to always think it would be harder going up something so steep."

William smiled and shook his head. "You certainly committed to it."

"Hard not to when you've got an army of those fuckers on your back." Olga finally turned to him. "Go big or go home, right?"

"Rig—" The words left William when they rounded the next bend. The space opened up to reveal a plaza of sorts. Although its massive grey walls made it look more like a medieval courtyard. They'd seen them from the top of the wall, but until that moment, they'd been walking along paths and roads. "What is this place?"

Two huge steel barns dominated the space. Each one large enough to accommodate hundreds of people. Lights shone from both of them, and chatter spilled out into the square. Loud because of the volume of people there rather than any noticeably raucous behaviour. The barns, although they shared the same plaza, faced away from one another. They stood side by side, diagonally in the square with their doors pointing in opposite directions. Light shone from each. The door for the one closest to William and Olga pointed at the plaza's far left corner. It showed them a way out.

Smaller dwellings lined the plaza's perimeter. Steel huts and tiny houses. They had windows and doors. Despite their cold exteriors, they were sturdy and no doubt well insulated. Certainly better than anything they'd had in Edin. Winters had been brutal back home. "We should go around," William said.

Olga grabbed his arm. "Wait."

"For what?"

"Look at the lights. They're only coming from the barns. All the houses are dark."

"So?"

"So, surely that means all the people here are either in one barn or the other. I reckon we can keep to the shadows and cut through this place unnoticed."

"Why don't we just go around?" And while they were at it, maybe they could widen their search for Matilda and the others.

"This is a much more direct route."

The enormous walls' shadows swamped the small dwellings lining the plaza's perimeter. It would keep them hidden. "You think it's worth it?"

"Don't you?"

"Why do you think they positioned the barns like that? Facing away from one another."

Olga shrugged. "Maybe it gives them a better view of what's coming into the square. What's the point of staring at one another while you have your back to a potential ambush?"

"Makes sense."

"So, are we going to do this?"

William's throat dried. Swallowing only made it worse. If they wanted to get to the building the guards had headed towards, it made sense to go through here. But what if Matilda and the others were closer? What if they were in trouble like his gut told him they were? What then? Surely they'd be better finding another way. Spending more time in the vicinity just in case they bumped into them.

"William?" Olga spoke with the hiss of muted impatience. She leaned closer to him and raised her eyebrows. "Well?"

What choice did they really have? A wild goose chase based on his feelings that would have them running through a place filled with strange vehicles, guards with guns, fire-breathing dogs, and heavily armed drones? Or a solid plan with purpose? They were surrounded by thousands, if not hundreds of thousands of people who hated them because they spoke the wrong language. They needed to get to the building, find their friends, and get out of here. "Okay."

Olga tutted. "Take longer next time if you like."

"It's not a simple choice. This place looks dangerous."

"As opposed to the paradise we've walked through until this moment?"

"Point taken."

Olga stepped towards the plaza's entrance. "You ready?"

"As I'll ever be."

"Don't put this on me. I need you to commit to this. Are you ready?"

William nodded. "Yes."

The second Olga entered the plaza, she turned left and walked alongside the outer wall. William followed.

The barn's doorway sent laughter out to them. Laughter and conversations in a language William didn't recognise. The rumble of hundreds of different people having hundreds of different conversations.

They remained close to the wall, hidden in its thick shadow. William snapped rigid when the chatter in the barn spiked. Both he and Olga spun towards the doorway. The light cast across the plaza changed, broken by people moving across it. But they stayed inside.

"Come on." Olga waved William forwards, leading him on a tiptoed run towards the plaza's first corner.

A sentry gun above her, she waited for William to catch up before pointing along the back of the small houses. "It's even darker behind them. I say we make a run for it and get through here as quickly as possible."

His heart pounding, his pulse throbbing in his ears, William nodded. Anything to get them out of there.

"Okay." Olga led the way across the backs of the small huts. Each dwelling faced into the plaza, the back walls of each building made from yet more windowless grey steel.

The gaps grew smaller as they progressed. The huts moved incrementally closer to the wall. They'd either started building them farther away and realised they could move them closer, or vice versa. Two different narratives depending on which side you started from. What did either matter? Soon they wouldn't have the space to run along the backs of the small buildings.

About three-quarters of the way across the square, William turned sideways to pass behind the next hut. The brushed steel of the rear of the building and the fifty-foot wall rubbed against his front and back. He grabbed Olga before she ran to the next one. "We have to go another way."

"We can get behind a few more."

"*You* can."

"Oh!" She looked him up and down. "Fair point. You can't do one more?"

"Not quietly."

"Okay, let's go across the front of them. Whatever they're doing in those barns, they look busy. And we're nearly there."

At the back of the next small hut, Olga dropped into a crouch and crawled under the window in its side wall. It hung open by an inch. She paused beneath it and pointed up.

William strained his ears. Heavy breathing inside. Panting. Groans.

Olga rolled her eyes. Not everyone had gone to the barn that evening. She led them on, across the front of the small house. The closed front door ensured the couple's private moment remained that way. If only they'd thought about the window too.

At the back wall again, William said, "I could have done without hearing that."

"I know, right?" Olga screwed up her face. "That was awkward. You ready for the next one?"

"As I'll …" William nodded. "Yes." She needed him to commit. "Yes, I am."

About ten more houses between them and their exit on the other side of the plaza. Ten more front doors. Ten more pairs of windows, one on each side of the small huts. Hopefully not ten more screwing couples.

They passed the next six like they had the one with the impassioned pair. The windows were open on all of them, but if there were people inside, they hid it well. Each of them had their front doors closed.

Olga halted when they ran across the front of the next hut, and William slammed into her. He fought the urge to shove her, instead throwing his hands out to the sides. "What are you doing?"

Pointing around the corner in the direction they were heading, Olga stepped back for William to see for himself. A man had stumbled from the next hut along. He'd wandered around the side to exactly where they intended to go. The man rested one hand against the back wall and groaned as he relieved himself. Steam rose from his stream of piss.

They were about as exposed as they could be to the barn. William gripped his sword's handle and chewed the inside of his mouth while he divided his attention between the pissing man and the barn's exit. If he had to cut him down to get out of there, then so be it.

Four to five hundred people inside the barn. They ate together, many of them quiet, heads bowed, getting on with it. They didn't come here to celebrate. They came here to feed.

The man returned to his hut. He walked with the clumsy gait of either intoxication or someone fresh from sleep. Either way, he moved with little consideration for his surroundings, closing the door behind him with a *click!*

Olga raised her eyebrows. Her cheeks puffed when she blew out. She pointed around the side of the hut, and William nodded, following her again.

The heady reek of fresh urine hung where the man had been.

Olga ruffled her nose. "He needs to drink more water."

They passed his hut and the next. Two more to go.

If the people in the barn were only there to eat, they'd be leaving soon. Many sat back, empty plates before them. Olga quickened her pace, and William followed.

Across the front of the next hut, William copied Olga by

walking on his tiptoes. The door opened beside him, and he froze. A small girl stood in the doorway. Her jaw fell loose as if mirroring William's plummeting stomach.

CHAPTER 10

Battered and bruised, Gracie lay on her side in the centre of the plaza and rocked with her ragged breaths. She wheezed from the kicking the boy had given her, but she'd won. They wouldn't goad her into stooping to their level. If they wanted to kill her, let the animals show their true colours. Bullies and savages, they didn't want a fight; they wanted a show. They wanted to make those watching on believe they weren't cold-blooded murders. To justify their killing of Gracie and her friends. But she wouldn't play the part they'd written for her.

The rough concrete felt cool against the side of Gracie's swollen face. It offered a little relief. A counterpoint to the buzzing prickly heat of her bruises. Her bleeding nose fed into an ever-growing pool.

Her friends remained in their cage about thirty feet away. The other prisoners watched on. Gaunt faces. Wide eyes. Were they next? Gracie shouted, "I won't let them drag me into their savage world. I won't lower myself. They're monsters. Surely you can see that now, Matilda?"

Matilda and Hawk, like the rest of the prisoners around

the plaza, pressed their faces to the gaps between the bars. Matilda, her brow creased, shrugged. "You know them better than me."

"Which is why I'm right. If they want to kill me, let them kill me defenceless. I won't allow them to hide from their own cowardice and lack of humanity."

Matilda shrugged again.

And why did Gracie need her approval, anyway? She could think what she wanted.

The boy stepped closer and loomed over Gracie. The shine from the plaza's floodlights hit his pale and gaunt face. His high cheekbones reflected the glare, his sallow cheeks and the bags beneath his eyes all the darker for the bright light. His cheeks glistened with his tears. Had he come here believing himself to be a hero? A champion? Believing himself to be something more than a pawn shoved into a battle by those who should have known better. People who should have cared more about his well-being. But they didn't give a shit about him. They didn't give a shit about anyone. Any belief he'd brought with him had well and truly gone. They'd sent him on a coward's mission. His fists trembled at his sides, and his chest rose and fell with his laboured breaths.

The rough ground scratched Gracie's face when she shook her head. "I won't fight you. I won't fight any of you."

Clack!

A guard opened Hawk and Matilda's cage. Five entered. Three were armed. Two carried spears and one a large and crude knife.

"Don't give in to them," Gracie said.

The guards tied Matilda's and Hawk's hands behind their backs.

"Their depravity knows no bounds." Gracie winced when the two thugs who'd previously pulled her to her feet stormed over, sent to her by the large woman with the wiry hair.

She dragged her knees towards her chest and curled into a ball, but the expected beating never came. Instead, they lifted her upright and stood her in front of the ragged boy, whose breaths gathered momentum, well on his way to a panic attack.

Gracie shuffled closer to him. His hot breath pressed against her face. She smiled through the waterfall of blood running over her lips and down her chin. "I know what you are. I know what you all are, and you won't beat me. If you want to kill me, then do it. But I won't give you the satisfaction of—"

"Argh!" Hawk stumbled, dragged from his cage and shoved by the guard with the knife. He fell face first against the ground. His hands bound, he lay on his front like a fish. He lifted his head. Glistening grazes streaked his cheek. "I won't let them drag me into a fight, Gracie."

Two more guards lifted Hawk like they'd lifted Gracie. At first, he let his legs go limp and fell to his knees. But when they lifted him a second time, another guard drove the wind from him with a hard blow to the stomach.

Hawk brayed like a donkey and leaned forward to pull air into his barking lungs.

Tears burned Gracie's eyes. Much easier to resist their violence when they levelled it at her.

One of the two men next to Gracie shouted.

"I don't know what—"

Crack!

The boy threw a hook, catching her left cheek. The men had been talking to him.

Her ears rang, her face throbbed, and a stinging electric buzz twinged through her with every movement. She stepped closer to the crying boy and shook with the force of her words. "You won't break me."

The men barked at the boy again, the large woman with the wiry hair shouting too.

The punch came from a mile away, but Gracie kept her hands at her sides.

Crack!

Gracie stumbled, but remained standing. She stamped her foot. "Fuck you!"

Hawk's boots scraped over the concrete when his two guards dragged him over and stood him in front of the boy. The wiry-haired woman shouted, and Gracie's stomach clamped when the boy hit Hawk.

Crack!

Hawk went down. Still winded, his hands still bound, he lay in a gasping heap.

"Are you all right?"

Hawk shook his head. "No. But don't give in to them, right? If you're certain they're going to kill us anyway, why allow them to justify their actions?"

Matilda remained tight-lipped. She'd also been dragged from the cage and had two spears and a rusty knife levelled at her.

Crack!

The boy punched Gracie again. She dropped to her knees on the hard and rough concrete.

The two large men bent down to lift her, and she hissed at them like a cat. She stood unaided and spat on the ground at the guards' feet before squaring up to the boy.

Crack!

Gracie went down again, her world spinning.

Crack!

The boy knocked Hawk over for a second time.

She could make the choice for herself when they were

only attacking her, but now they were taking it out on a bound Hawk ... Gracie propped herself up on one hand. "What shall I do, Hawk? Shall I fight back?"

"Yes!" Matilda said.

Before Hawk replied, one of the two large men gagged him by dragging a cloth around the bottom half of his face and pulling it tight across his mouth. Snot and blood shot from his nose while he bit down on the rag. His eyes widened, and his nostrils flared. He mumbled a reply.

"I don't know what you're—"

Crack!

The boy knocked Gracie flat again.

The man with the crude knife left Matilda's side.

One of Hawk's guards clamped his hand across his brow and pulled his head back, forcing him to stare at the night sky, exposing his scarred throat.

Matilda shouted, "Gracie! Do something!"

The man raised his rusty blade to Hawk's throat. He dragged it up against the scars, digging deep enough to draw blood.

The rag muted Hawk's screams.

Gracie stumbled to her feet again and walked to the boy, who shook like he had hypothermia.

The large woman shouted.

Gracie jumped back, avoiding the boy's wild swing. She countered with a hard jab to his chin.

The skinny boy flopped, and she rushed him. She kicked him while he lay on the ground. "This was what you wanted, wasn't it?" A red-mist spray of spittle filled the air in front of her. "Someone to give you a kicking so you and your spineless people can pretend they're acting in self-defence when they kill us all." She kicked him again and again. "Well, here it is, you piece of shit!" Her next kick missed when the two men dragged her away.

Twisting free from their tight grip, Gracie ran at the boy again. He groaned and writhed on the ground. She kicked him in the face.

Clop!

The boy fell limp.

The two men grabbed her harder this time. They dragged her back towards her cage.

The large, wiry-haired woman sneered.

"Isn't that what you wanted? For us to fight back?"

The two men threw Gracie into the cage. She stumbled, tripped, and landed on her side. The coppery flow of her own blood still ran down the back of her throat. They threw Hawk and Matilda in after her. She crawled over to Hawk. "Are you okay?"

Nodding several times, Hawk wheezed and lifted his head, his hands still tied behind his back. The deep cut on his throat ran about eight inches long and glistened under the glare of the floodlights. "Yeah. I'm sorry you had to fight them."

"Sometimes you have to try a different approach if one way isn't working," Matilda said.

"That's easy for you to say. All you did was watch."

"Because that's what they chose for me. And they didn't kill you when you fought back, did they?"

Gracie turned away from her, her jaw tight. "That doesn't mean they won't. Don't mistake this lot for human beings."

CHAPTER 11

The small girl mirrored William's expression. Wide-eyed, slack-jawed, and yet to scream. Her mouth worked as if she could find the words to make this situation better. She wore a raggedy brown dress and clung to a doll made from sticks and bound with twine.

William could run, but what if she shouted? He could shove her back inside and slam the door shut. Lock her in. At least mute her calls for help. It would give them the head start they so desperately needed. He could reason with her. He wrapped his right hand around his sword's hilt. Olga gasped, and the girl's wide eyes darted to his gesture. He loosened his grip. Not an option.

Olga crouched down in front of the girl. She held her hands. "It's okay."

The girl screamed.

The wild squeal of a distressed pig. She released it in shrill waves.

Ice streaked through William. He threw up his arms. "Now she knows we're the enemy."

The hum of conversation in the hall died.

Every person looked their way. "Shit!" William said. "Run!"

Olga led their escape. They'd been just feet from their exit. Just feet from passing through the plaza unnoticed. And they might have made it had Olga not revealed who they were by speaking the language of their enemy.

The light of the plaza at their backs, they pushed on into the dark maze.

Olga slowed down at a fork in the road.

"Just take any path!" William sprinted past her down the dark road on the right.

"What if it doesn't lead to the guards' building?"

"I don't give a shit where it leads as long as it gets us out of here."

"I'm sorry, William. I'm sorry I blew our cover." The tight tunnel added an echo to Olga's whimper.

"Being sorry doesn't help right now."

The tight roads and tall walls amplified the chasing army's steps. The barn had had hundreds of people inside. No doubt the other one had been as packed. Had both of them emptied? William took the left path at the next fork.

The hammering steps grew louder. They knew this place, and it would take more than the darkness to slow them down. "Shit!"

Twenty to thirty people blocked the road ahead. Men and women, they stood in the weak moonlight and held a variety of weapons, from sticks to clubs to knives.

Crack!

William avoided the first launched rock.

Crack!

Another one.

A thick white line about one hundred feet behind the mob. William turned right, away from the roadblock and away from the line.

Those at the roadblock gave chase. They added to the number on their tail. Thousands yet? It certainly sounded like it.

Several quick turns, William took every one at the last moment. Too dark to plan ahead. A wider path opened up for them. Another thick white line lay across the road. Another target for them to reach. Although, what good would it do to cross a line? What would it achieve?

"Jeez!" Olga said.

A shot of adrenaline speared William's gut. Another mob appeared ahead. Fifteen to twenty people. They blocked the path as effectively as the previous lot.

The chasing pack's front runners caught up, closing in from behind. The shadows hid what would no doubt be twisted grimaces of hate. Hundreds of faceless silhouettes with more appearing from multiple paths. They'd swarmed through this maze. They had the numbers to close off every route.

"We can't stay here." Olga led them right, and William followed.

The next long and straight path. The next white line, now only fifty feet away. The next mob to close them off. With every subsequent roadblock, they'd faced fewer soldiers. Only fifteen this time. About ten of them carried rocks.

Fifty-foot steel walls on either side. Hundreds of people behind. Olga shook her head. "We've got nowhere to go. We're not getting out of here."

The army behind closed in. The group ahead swayed from side to side. More rocks than clubs, but they were ready for war.

William battled his ragged breaths. Sweat burned his tired eyes. He sidled next to Olga and spoke from the side of his mouth. Not that they'd understand what he said. "We need to get past that white line."

"How do you know?"

"I don't. But unless you have a better suggestion, I'd say it's worth a try."

"So how do we get past?"

The army behind slowed. Cautious in their approach despite their numbers. Packed shoulder to shoulder between the huge steel walls, they carried a variety of weapons, which they raised as they edged closer. They were in control here. They didn't need to rush in and risk injury to themselves.

William's sword rang when he drew it. The resonating blade gave those behind them pause. Olga drew hers.

"Most of them have rocks," William said. "This is our best chance of getting past."

William's scream echoed as he charged. "Come on!"

Olga ran beside him and rolled her tongue with a shrill war cry. The old Olga. The one who needed more than an army between her and a way out to stop her. There would only ever be one winner, and the sooner they accepted it, the less suffering they'd have to endure.

William dodged the first launched rock. It bounced off the concrete floor, skittering into those on their tail.

Several more rocks. Several more adjustments to avoid the attack. One or two of them rang against the steel walls.

Leading with the tip of his sword, Olga doing the same beside him, William zeroed in on one soldier holding a club. She screamed a moment before he stabbed her in the chest. The man beside her fell from Olga's attack.

Hands grabbed at William, but he forced them back with a wild slash.

Olga tripped and stumbled, but she remained on her feet.

Both of them broke clear of the mob and crossed the white line.

The road open ahead, William sped up. How long before

their route got closed off again? Before another mob blocked their path. Before those behind—

"Wait!" Olga halted and pointed back from where they'd just come. She panted with the effort of their escape. "They've stopped."

"I knew it!" William punched his hand. "I knew those lines meant something. They can't cross them."

The army gathered behind the white line. They stood at least ten feet from it. They launched rocks at William and Olga. Some of them threw their clubs and blades. The projectiles slammed to the ground between them. Very few of the soldiers had the strength to launch them as far as they needed.

William flipped them the bird. The soldiers shouted and yelled. They punched the air, weapons in hand. More rocks crashed down against the concrete. An ineffective attack from an impotent army.

"I guess that gesture crossed the language barrier, then?" Olga said.

Unable to suppress his smile, William snorted a laugh. "Come on, let's get out of here."

CHAPTER 12

The glow from Joni's screens guided her back down the ladder. They ran a blue-hued highlight across the top of each cold steel rung. The shine countered the deep shadows from the massive building she'd just left. Being anywhere near the gigantic block at night cast you into a darkness deeper than the devil's soul.

"You can stop moaning now. Joni has some food for you." Not that he'd hear her through the thick steel door. But when he saw the food, he'd shut up. He'd know that she looked after him. "Well, he'd best shut up. *I'm hungry. I'm hungry.* Like a baby bird that should have been shoved from the nest before it learned to fly. Joni will feed him, but so help him if he still complains." Her heart galloped. She clenched her jaw. "Joni's a patient woman, but even she has her limits."

Joni jumped from the ladder a few rungs before she reached the ground. The slap of her dismount whipped around her small home. The *crack* of the soles of her shoes against damp concrete. "So he's quiet now? Joni risks her life to get him food, and he suddenly decides he isn't hungry?"

Rusty flakes clung to Joni's palms. She wiped them off on her trousers. She slipped her bag from her back and opened the zip. The deer meat nestled amongst the veg. She took a bite for herself. Her mouth watered with each gamey chew. Rich and earthy. She used her tongue to push the chunk into her left cheek. "He'd best appreciate what Joni's done for him. Otherwise there will be trouble. And no one likes to see Joni angry. You hear me?" Her voice echoed in the cavernous underground space. The walls dark with damp. The funk of mould hung in the air. "You'd best show me your gratitude."

The thick steel door must have muted his reply. His acquiescence. Joni knew best. Let her speak and accept what she had to give. Unless … "Maybe he can't hear Joni? But Joni hears him. *I'm hungry! I'm hungry.*" Some of the meat flew from her mouth, spat against the steel door with the force of her words. "I'm hungry!"

Joni rocked and shook her head. She knocked against her temple. "He's allowed to be hungry. Joni needs to calm down. Relax. Take a chill pill." She walked in circles. "She can't go in there like this. All riled and furious. Let him be hungry. Joni will take care of him. His number one fan. She'll show him how well she looks after someone. Yes." She nodded. "Treat him right. Be kind. Be considerate."

The chunk of deer meat in her grip, the key to unlock the door in her other hand, Joni chewed on her mouthful of meat, slipped the key into the lock, and turned it, the action gritty. *Crack!*

The steel door's hinges groaned. The room stretched away from her. A small light in the corner. Like a child who feared the dark, she'd given him a nightlight for comfort. "Joni knows how to care for people."

Strapped to her wheeled board's trailer like she'd left him. "We can't have him getting away now, can we? Hey." She crossed the room. "Joni's brought you some food." She leaned over him. "You said you were hungry, so Joni's providing. Got you some meat. Protein. It's good for you. Will help you feel better. Heal better. Seal better. No." She knocked her head. "You're not the one who's been cut. That's not you."

He remained still.

Joni slowed her approach. She walked on tiptoes, ready to jump back. He wouldn't catch her off guard. "Is this a trick?"

He lay still, strapped to his trolley like when she'd left him. Unconscious. Or, at least, pretending to be. "Wake up!"

He breathed. In and out. Slow and steady. Alive. Unconscious.

Joni placed the food on the trolley and leaned over him. She frowned. "You kept saying you were hungry." She scratched her head. "Look, I get you're upset, but Joni will look after you. She will care for you. Joni provides. Look." She held up the meat. "Joni *has* provided."

"Hey!" Joni pressed her finger into his cheek. It sank into his soft flesh. "Hey!" She pressed again. "Wake up!"

Joni's pulse sped, and she slapped him. *Crack!*

She pulled her hand away and clasped it to her chest. "Joni doesn't do that. No. No-no-no-no-no. That's not Joni's way."

She raised her hand again. But she held it this time. "You need to talk to her. She gets it, you're upset. And you have every right to be."

He remained still.

"Where's that little chick gone? That little chirping bird. *I'm hungry. I'm hungry.* Cheep, cheep! Mama Bird's here to feed the chick. To help you grow big and strong so you can fly. Leave the nest." Still chewing on a piece of meat, Joni reached into her mouth and pinched off a chunk. It glistened with her saliva. "This is how a mama looks after the chicks." She rolled the meat into a small ball. "She goes away from the nest and comes back with food in her mouth. Already chewed for you. The love a mama has for her little ones. Mama will feed you. You'll be ready to fly in no time."

Joni pressed the pellet of meat into his mouth. It squished against his face. She lifted his top lip in a pinch and forced it in with her other finger, a bar of dirt beneath her nails. The meat between his lips and teeth, she stuffed more in. "There we go." She beamed a grin. "This is how a mama looks after her chicks." She pulled another small chunk from her mouth and stuffed it in after the first. A small bulge where it sat. Ready to eat later on. When she left. When he didn't need to pretend to be unconscious. "We'll get you big and strong and ready to leave the nest in no time."

Joni left the room. She grinned like she hadn't in a long time. She'd been born to care for people. They'd lucked out that she'd been the one to find them. It would have been so much different if they'd fallen into his hands. "Don't worry, little one, Mama's here. Mama will look after you for as long as you need protecting. While Mama's in charge, you'll come to no harm."

CHAPTER 13

The wind ran across the open square, gathering up the chill from the concrete ground, steel walls, and icy glares from the prisoners in the other cages. It threw it all in Gracie's throbbing face. It also found the patch of exposed skin at the base of her back. The patch where she'd torn a strip of fabric from her shirt. The strip hung from her grip and flapped in the wind. She held it in Hawk's direction. "For your throat."

"No." He showed her the palm of his right hand while he gripped his throat with his left. Gracie had untied him and Matilda the second the guards had left them alone in the cage. "I don't need it."

The blue fabric danced in the breeze. "What else will I do with it? I've already torn it off."

Hawk reached towards her, paused, and took the piece of her shirt. He wrapped it around his neck like a cravat and nodded while he tied it at the back. "Thank you."

"Welcome. Hopefully it will stop an infection." The floodlights' interrogating glare exposed every uncovered prisoner in every cage around the plaza's perimeter. Guards worked their way from one cage to the next, tossing large sheets over them, throwing the prisoners into darkness like they were animals that needed to go to sleep for the night. How had they all ended up here? Did they get dragged from their cage and attacked like Gracie had been?

The cloth around Hawk's neck glistened from where the blood had already soaked through. "Thanks for going against your wishes. I don't think they would have stopped if you hadn't fought back."

Gracie shrugged. "I didn't want to do it."

"Which is why I'm grateful. If we ever get out of here—"

"*When* we get out of here." Matilda glanced behind, but the guards throwing the sheets over the cages still had a way to go before they reached them.

Hawk tilted his head to one side. "*If* we ever get out of here, I'm going to have to think long and hard about returning north. When we were there, it seemed like a shitty place. But then w—"

"—we came here." Gracie raised her eyebrows.

"Right."

About half an hour had passed since Gracie fought the boy. If it could be called a fight. About half an hour had passed since Gracie had shown him what happened when she punched back. He'd earned her retaliation. But she'd walked away with the more severe injuries. If she moved her head too quickly, it stung her swollen face. Even the wind from the wrong angle lit up her skin. If he came back for another fight, she wouldn't let him hurt her again. Although he seemed like as much of a victim as her. Forced into battle by those nasty bastards running this place. Why were they torturing their own? "If these monsters let us go," Gracie said, "it'll be a miracle. Although, I don't understand why they're toying with us. How long do you think it will be before they get bored and decide to kill us? I'm gues—"

A woman emerged from the path closest to them. She carried an axe, the blade as crude as the knife they'd used to cut Hawk's throat. Handmade. Hand-beaten. Hand-sharpened. But also hand-operated. If she swung it hard enough, it'd take off a head. Even if it took multiple attempts.

"Here we go!" Electric streaks ran up either side of Gracie's face when she opened and closed her jaw. She'd fight back if they tried to kill them. "It must be why they're covering the cages. They don't want the others to see what they're going to do to us."

Matilda stood on Gracie's left and Hawk on her right. Hawk said, "What's that sound?"

Those parts of the square that were untouched by the floodlights stood extra dark in comparison. The path closest to them, the path the woman had emerged from, appeared so black that when Gracie stared into it, it sucked the light from her brain. It hid whatever made the *whoosh* from being dragged across concrete.

"What are they doing?" Matilda said.

The hairs on the back of Gracie's arms stood on end. "So you want my advice now?"

"I'm not here to oppose everything you say, Gracie. If I have a different opinion, I'll voice it."

"If you think I'm wrong, you mean?"

"That tends to be what a difference of opinion is. And if you weren't so defensive, you might actually listen to what other people had to say."

The guards had covered about half of the cages in the plaza. "You don't know these people like I do. You'd do well to trust my experience."

"And I do. But that doesn't mean I can ignore your biases."

"Mattresses," Hawk said.

"Biases," Matilda said.

"No." Hawk pointed at the dark tunnel. "Mattresses."

Thunk! The woman with the axe opened the cage's lock. She pulled the door wide and entered first. Three people followed her in, each one dragging a mattress.

Another three people entered as those who'd dragged in the mattresses left. They each carried an armful of clean blankets. They dropped them on each mattress, all of them avoiding eye contact as if they were subservient to Gracie, Matilda, and Hawk.

The last person in the procession wheeled in a trolley carrying three plates of food and three cups of water. He handed one of each to Matilda and Hawk. Gracie nearly shoved her plate back, but her body spoke for her. Her stomach rumbled, her mouth watered, and her hands took the gift. Her jaw hung loose while the man with the trolley left. The woman with the axe followed him out and locked the cage's door again. *Thunk.*

Hawk sat and pressed his hands down on either side of him. "What's in these mattresses?"

Gracie sat too. Soft. Spongy. "I dunno. But certainly not old rags or straw." And the sheets were thick and clean. "It's a trick. These people don't have kindness in them. There's a catch to these gifts."

Matilda spoke with her mouth full. "You don't know that."

"You should think yourself lucky that you don't see my perspective."

"I see it. But that doesn't mean I won't challenge it."

"You've not seen what I have." Pointing her thumb at her own chest, Gracie's tired eyes itched, and her voice warbled. "I've seen people hunted down like they were wild animals." She pointed outside the cage at the path the people had emerged from. "I've seen those savages laugh while they killed Dout's citizens. I've seen unspeakable cruelty, so don't tell me what I do and don't know."

"You were at war."

"What do you know about war?"

"I know it makes people do awful things to one another. Fear makes people react in horrible ways. Besides, the Gracie who brought us to Dout still had compassion and empathy. She still wanted to find another way."

"That was before they attacked my home. Before they killed my dad and brother."

"What would the people from the communities close to Dout say about you lot? About Aus?"

"Don't you dare."

"Gracie, I'm on your side, I really am. But you're losing your head here. We're in a different situation to the one you were in in Dout."

"We're in a fucking *cage,* Matilda. We're being held as prisoners."

"You're right."

"Huh?"

"You're right," Matilda said. "While they might not be torturing us, and while they've apparently rewarded us for fighting back, rather than killing us like you thought they would—"

"This isn't over yet!"

"—I agree, we are still their prisoners," Matilda said. "I don't want to argue with you. Especially not after what you did to try to go after Artan with me. You risked your life backing my poorly thought-out plan. Thank you again for that."

The heat from the stew warmed the plate and made Gracie's fingers tingle.

Matilda ate a spoonful. She bit into the small loaf of bread, tearing a chunk away with her teeth. Speaking with her mouth full, she raised the bread in Gracie's direction. "I obviously want to find a way out of here as much as you both do, but whatever happens, we might as well accept the food and bed. I'd rather be comfortable and fed than not."

Like Matilda, Hawk had tucked into his food. He chewed on the bread and sat with one of the thick blankets wrapped around his shoulders.

Gracie's stomach rumbled. The stew's rich smell snaked up her nostrils. The prisoners in the few cages yet to be covered pressed their faces to the bars. They hadn't been given food and blankets. They hadn't been given mattresses. They stared across the plaza with murderous intent. Matilda didn't know these people like Gracie did. In her quest to play devil's advocate, she'd gone blind to their surroundings. Just look at how they treated their own. But that didn't make her wrong about everything. If they were going to die anyway, probably at the hands of the other furious prisoners, they might as well do it on a full stomach and after a good night's sleep.

The gamey deer tasted like home. Of eating with her dad while they talked about Dout and what they could do to keep it safe. While they planned a future that would never come. She swallowed past the lump in her throat and laid her hand on her chest. Her mum and dad's wedding rings pressed into her palm. If only she had them with her now. What advice would they give her? She bit into the bread. They'd tell her to eat. Matilda didn't know these people. She'd soon come to see them for the savages they are, but it made no sense to abstain from food and sleep. And it made no sense to argue. Gracie toasted her friends with the small chunk of bread before she took another bite. And she'd best eat it while she could still see. The guards with the sheets were working their way closer. It wouldn't be long before they were also sitting in enforced darkness.

CHAPTER 14

The sky had turned from black to dark blue to a lighter shade of blue as night gave way to morning. The rising sun on their left confirmed they were still heading south. Dew clung to every steel surface like perspiration. William hugged himself and shivered. "But at least we're free."

Her jaw tight, her nose red, Olga folded her arms across her chest, twisting into herself. She scowled at him. "Huh?"

"At least we're free. It might be cold and miserable, but things could have been a lot worse."

"How did you know about the white lines? That we needed to cross them?"

"I didn't. Not really. But they had to mean something, right?" William shrugged, dragging his feet as he walked. "Otherwise, why are they there?"

They came to another open area. Sentry guns were dotted along the walls around the perimeter. But were they anything more than ornaments? Were they just there to add to the aesthetic? A reminder that someone else had control? Maybe he shouldn't get too complacent. If the lines meant something, he should apply that same logic to these guns.

A scattering of buildings throughout the square. Larger than the houses they'd come across, but nothing compared to the huge barns. "This looks like some kind of industrial space. Like they make things here."

Olga approached something that looked like a cross between a trolley and a wheelbarrow. Filled with identical pieces of steel, she picked one out. They were semicircles with eight holes equally spaced around their single curved edge. She lifted one towards the sky and peered through it. "What do you think they use these for?"

"Who knows? But they must be important if they're making so many."

Another trolley had steel rods that were all exactly the same size. About three feet long, they were heavy and well balanced. Were it not for his sword, William might have taken one. Instead, he dropped it back in with the others with a clatter. "I can't stop thinking about those white lines."

Olga shrugged. "What about them in particular?"

"We now know the people won't cross them, but we don't know why. And have Matilda and the others worked it out yet? What if they don't know that getting across the lines means safety? What if they've been chased like we were? What if they get blocked off like we did? What if they only need to cross a line and they don't know that? What if they've been captured? What if we're close to them now?"

"The second you give up ..."

"I know it sounds like bullshit, but what if I'm right?"

Olga raised her eyebrows as they continued through the industrial space. Too early for people to be starting work.

"For most of my life," William said, "I've had Matilda's back, and she's had mine. There was this one time at school." He smiled. "We had a big dumb kid in our class called Adam Slate. Gormless bastard. He empowered himself by trying to be the big man. He had nothing else going for him. One day, he turned on me. Tried to start a fight because he'd had a particularly humiliating day at school. It was quite sad, really. He never understood anything, and the teachers would often loose patience with him. Whether they meant to, they'd humiliate him, which meant someone at school would get it. But it was hard to see him as a victim back then. Especially when he turned his frustrations on you and the people you cared about."

"So what happened?"

William laughed and shook his head. "He was shouting at me. Goading me. Quite a crowd had gathered. I didn't know what to do. I was only eight and not much of a fighter. He was saying horrible things about me. About my family." His fists balled, but what could he do? Take a swing at the past? Change the indelible narrative? Fight back? "Before I could punch him, Matilda appeared from out of nowhere and cracked him on the chin. Unlike me, she knew violence. She had no fear. At least, not from her peers. What could an eight-year-old do to her?"

"What happened to Adam?"

"He went down like an empty grain sack. Matilda kicked him in the stomach and walked away. From that day on, we called her *the one-bang.*"

"And that didn't work against you? A girl fighting your battles?"

"Matilda and I have always been a team. You start a fight with one, you get a fight with both. Everyone knew that. If anything, it strengthened our bond and kept people off our backs. We've always looked out for one another. We've never given up on one another either." They passed several more trolleys holding more strange parts, but none of them made any sense or appeared to be of any use on their own. William led Olga down a path on the other side. The acoustics of his voice changed with the closer steel walls. "I still can't shake the feeling that if wc give up, we'll be giving up on them. That building the guards went towards is a long way away. A lot could happen between here and there."

"So we don't go?"

They crossed another painted white line. Two large glass lights on the walls on either side. "No." William shook his head. "I still think we should go, but maybe we should do it in a more roundabout way? What if Matilda and the others have been caught and they're close? We could search this area a little more *while* we head for the block."

"This place is dangerous."

The siren to signal the opening gates sounded in the distance. It cut through the sedate morning. A moaning and wailing catcall. The diseased would be closing in on the front of the place right now. How many people were they about to send to their death?

"I want to make sure Matilda and the others are okay," William said.

"Whenever I have a tough decision, I ask myself what my sisters would do." Olga's eyes glazed. She smiled. "They had this strange symbiosis that made them greater than the sum of their parts. They could counter one another's perspectives and often arrive at the best course of action. Each was wonderful in their own right, but together they were formidable. I try to replicate their discussions. To carry both of their voices in my head."

"What do they say about our current situation?"

Olga hesitated.

"Just say it, Olga. You think it's a bad idea? *They* think it's a bad idea?"

Olga threw an arm across William. "Wait!" She dragged him back. She'd stopped him from entering another industrial space. There were already people in there. "They don't look like they've turned up to work."

A group of six. Four men and two women. Dressed in rags, they ran into the square's centre, pushing a wheeled, towering catapult. Its base was a rectangular steel frame with steel wheels on the corners, each one about three feet in diameter. The apex of the catapult's pivot stood about ten feet tall. One end of the long arm, the shorter end, had sandbags attached to it. The other end had a large basket and a taut rope holding it in place against the weight of the sandbags. The six people filled the basket with parts similar to the ones William and Olga had found in the trolleys.

A humming sound behind them pulled William around. "Shit!" It came from the road they were on.

Olga grabbed his sleeve and dragged him just inside the industrial space, towards the people with the catapult. They hid in the gap between one of the many buildings and the steel wall.

Two guards entered the plaza. A man and a woman. Each stood on something similar to the thing the woman who'd kidnapped Artan and Nick drove. A wheeled board minus the handlebars. They both had a gun hanging from a strap across their chest.

The people cried out.

The guards opened fire.

The people took cover behind the catapult and dropped in several more steel parts.

One pulled the lever, and the rope snapped. *Thwomp!* The heavy sandbags dragged the arm and basket over. It launched the steel pieces, the catapult rolling forwards and back again, eating up the momentum of the swinging arm.

William's mouth fell wide as the scattered parts sailed over their heads. Impossibly high, they flew towards the external wall.

Several sentry guns burst to life, activated by the flying steel. They released a stream of red-hot bullets that tinged off some of the small pieces. It disrupted their line of flight, spinning them and dropping them to the ground. But, for every piece that fell, five continued towards the external wall.

The guards fired on the fleeing group. A stuttered burst, much like the sentry guns. They hit the steel walls and buildings. They hit the catapults' frame. One of the six screamed, but the buildings blocked William's line of sight to them.

The guards jumped from their wheeled boards and ran deeper into the plaza.

William and Olga edged closer to their way out of there. Back the way they came.

The two guards laid into the person they'd shot. He crawled away like a slug, his legs bleeding and limp behind him. They kicked him, stamped on his injured legs, and slammed the butts of their guns into the back of his head. The force of the blows bounced his face off the concrete.

William's pulse sped, his words breathy. He grabbed Olga before she ran from cover. "Shall we?"

"Shall we what?"

He nodded at the wheeled boards and grinned.

"But how do we drive them?"

"How hard can it be?"

"Famous last words."

"Think about how much ground we'll be able to cover on those things. We'll be able to search this area *and* get to the building, all in the time it would have taken us to get to the building. This way, we can do what we both want. I know you're not into the idea of us searching for the others—"

"I didn't say that."

"You didn't need to. But surely this gives us the best of both plans, right?"

One guard yelled and jumped on the man's already damaged legs. He landed with the gut-wrenching *crack*.

The man's scream damn near shook the walls.

"We don't have long to decide."

Olga nodded. "Okay."

"You're sure?"

"Yeah, let's do this." Olga led the way, breaking from the cover of the building.

"Oi!" A guard aimed his gun at her. He shot, but the catapult shielded them from fire.

Olga jumped on the board, spun on the spot several times, and zipped out of there, back the way they'd come.

William, a step behind her, jumped on his board. Concrete chips sprayed his legs and sides from where the guards shot behind and in front of him. The steel walls sang with bullet fire. He went into a spin like Olga had. The board reacted to his pressure. Gravity pulled on his weight, leaning him into his rapid turn. He spun faster. He couldn't pull out of it. The micro-glimpses of the guards on each rotation showed them closing in. Guns raised. "Olg—"

She'd already gone.

CHAPTER 15

The light from a new day stung Gracie's eyes. She blinked to make sense of the silhouette leaning over her. She rubbed her face, lighting up every nerve ending on her swollen skin.

"Are you okay?" Matilda raised her eyebrows. "Still hurts?"

Of course it still hurt. This was all part of their plan to cause as much pain and suffering as they could before they killed them. What would have happened if she'd fought back straight away like Matilda had suggested? Would they still have fed them and given them blankets and mattresses? Would she have gone through enough torture to get the reward on the other side? Or would Gracie have saved a kicking had she listened to her in the first place?

"Gracie?" Matilda said.

"Sorry." Gracie still frowned to block out the sun. "It does. It really hurts. But I slept well last night. And bruising heals." Not that she'd be alive long enough to get through it. None of them would. But Matilda wouldn't hear any of it. "I'll be okay. For now."

"Good. Sorry to wake you, but they brought us some more food this morning." Matilda produced a white plate from behind her back. It had a bread roll, an apple, and a small brown bar.

Gracie pointed at the bar. "What's that?"

Matilda's eyes glowed, and she beamed with a grin. "It tastes *amazing*."

"What is it?"

"I don't know, but I've tasted nothing like it. Try it."

The uniformity of the bar made it look more like a machine part or a tiny brick. How could anything like this be worth eating? "Where are yours?"

Hawk sat on his mattress nearby. He clung to a bread roll from which he'd taken a bite. He spoke with his mouth full. "We've eaten ours already. I couldn't stop after one taste."

Her hands clasped in front of her chest, Matilda's already wide grin stretched even wider when Gracie lifted the bar and took the smallest bite. Sweeter than any fruit, it melted in her mouth. The sugary goo spread across her tongue. "It tastes a bit like honey."

"But soooo much better, right?"

Gracie smiled and dragged in another sharp breath. Her face didn't have joy in it yet. She took another bite and nodded as it melted again. "So much better. My god, what is it? We need to find out what it's called so we can get more. It's won—"

Until that moment, Gracie had forgotten where they were. In one cage of many, she and Matilda had been giggling and going on about the food they'd received, but the new day revealed the wide eyes, sallow cheeks, and sneering faces of the people in the other cages. The sheets had been removed. All the other prisoners were dirty, skinny, and desperate to tear into the three of them. They were living a life of luxury by comparison, and they had the gall to gloat about it. "Do you think we're the only ones to receive these bars and food?"

"Maybe?" Hawk took another bite of his bread and looked out across the plaza. "Maybe they've fed those on the other side? It's hard to tell from here."

Another bite. Gracie covered her mouth and lowered her voice. "I think we'd do well to hide our enjoyment. They already hate us; we could do with not making it any worse."

Matilda's smile fell, and Hawk dropped his head. The fabric around his neck had crusted with his dried blood. At least the bleeding had stopped.

A group of people strode into the plaza from the opposite side, led by the big woman with mousy-brown hair. She had three guards, each one taller and wider than her. The prisoners recoiled at her proximity like scared animals. They stared at the ground, reliving their trauma. They knew her levels of cruelty. And this was what she did to her own people. If only Matilda and Hawk had the same fear. But how could they? They'd not lived Gracie's life. And no matter how many stories she'd told them, how could they truly understand the depths of these people's depravity?

Another teenage boy walked behind the large woman. Another reluctant fighter. Her heavy stride beat slamming steps against the ground. He shuffled along with a bowed head.

"You know what they're doing to us, don't you?"

Crumbs sprayed from Hawk's mouth when he spoke. "They want us to fight again."

"Yeah, that." Gracie nodded out of the cage. "But see how all the other prisoners are looking at us? They're trying to make them resentful. When they're finished making us fight these little boys, the prisoners will be our next opponents. But before that happens, they'll make sure they fill them with as much hatred as they can. I say the more we comply, the closer we are to that happening."

Thunk! The woman unlocked the cage, sneered as she pulled the door wide, and pointed at Matilda.

Matilda shoved her own thumb into her chest as if to question the woman.

The woman's lips tightened, and she pointed at her again, the second jab delivered with greater force.

Gracie fought the urge to grab her friend when Matilda stepped forwards. She slumped where she sat. "One step closer."

The woman led Matilda into the centre of the plaza. Many of the prisoners stirred. Some shouted. Some banged on their cages. Some of them paced back and forth, so enraged they couldn't keep still. Every one watched Matilda, their eyes dark with sleep deprivation and starvation. They'd cut her throat given half a chance.

Gracie shook her head. "This will not end well."

"You think they want her to fight?" Hawk said.

The boy they'd brought with them rolled his shoulders and raised his fists. He snapped his neck from side to side.

Hawk said, "You think she'll fight back?"

"I hope not. Give them what they want and whatever they have planned for us will come much sooner. All we have right now is resistance, which will hopefully give us time to figure out how we're going to get out of here."

"But they fed us after you fought back. Where did resisting get you?"

"They gave me a beating first. What if Matilda doesn't take a kicking? You don't know these people like I do. This is all part of an elaborate game designed to do nothing but provide them with entertainment. They're giving us hope so they can break us later."

The lead woman stood between Matilda and the skinny

boy. She raised her thick arm, her clenched fist thrust at the cloudy sky. She looked at the boy.

He nodded.

She looked at Matilda, who also nodded.

The woman snapped her arm down between them and stepped back.

The boy charged.

Matilda kept her arms at her sides.

"Good girl," Gracie said. "Don't give them the sat—"

Matilda stepped right, dodged the boy's attack, and caught him with a hard blow to the chin on his way past. *Crack!*

The boy ran for several more wobbly steps, his knees buckling, his ankles twisting. He hit the ground, knees first, and catapulted onto the hard concrete, his forehead connecting with a *tonk!*

The woman shouted in a language Gracie recognised but didn't understand. She leaned over the unconscious boy, spraying him with spittle. Her face glowed red.

"Shit!" Gracie said. "We've just given them what they want."

Hawk remained on his mattress, his jaw hanging open mid-chew.

"All Matilda's done is speed up the punishment. And believe me, it's coming. We're screwed."

CHAPTER 16

The tight maintenance shaft took Joni's whispers and threw them away from her. "Joni knew it wouldn't take her long. She always finds him in the end." Laughter bubbled in her throat. "And she's getting better at it now. It used to take her weeks. He has to learn that no matter where he goes, Joni will always find him. Always."

Still asleep in his bed. His bed nowhere near the grate Joni peered through. She smiled. "It always happens. Whenever Joni drops something on him, like water, drip, drip, it always happens. He moves his bed, but Joni's smarter than that. Joni has other ways to get to him. So many other ways. He'll have to do more than rearrange the furniture. Oh, I do like what you've done with the place."

She rapped her knuckles against the side of her head. "Focus, Joni. He's still sleeping. He must have been doing the night shift. For once." She spoke through gritted teeth and sprayed spittle. "The selfish prick doesn't usually do nights. Has he wronged someone? Is he trying to make it up to them? What could he have possibly done to feel remorse? Does he even have remorse in him?"

The bottle of bleach shook in Joni's trembling hand. Taken from their very own supplies. Scarred by their own stock. "Whatever he's done, he has to pay. Oh yes, he has to pay."

Crawling along the hard steel maintenance shaft hurt Joni's knees and elbows. She moved to the next room along and pressed her face to the cold bars. "Empty. No one wants to be next to him. They don't want to get close to such a vile creature. And Joni can't blame them. She only wants to get close so she can hurt him. Again and again. Otherwise, she wouldn't even want to share the same building. The same planet. The same solar system. Vile man. Horrible little toad."

Empty plastic boxes filled the room below. "His boxes from moving? The room's empty. An easy one to drop into."

Joni rolled onto her back and stamped down on the grate. *Crash!*

The sound clattered through the maintenance tunnels.

Her heart beating in her throat, Joni shook her head. "No. Joni's made too much noise. Fucked it now. She'll have to come back another time. Another day."

The hatch's hinges squeaked as it swung. Joni rolled onto her front again, the steel cold against her stomach. She reached down and grabbed the grate. She tugged it towards her to pull it closed, but paused. "No sound. No footsteps. No alarm." A tilt of her head to one side. "Has no one heard? Is he truly alone on this floor? Is everyone else working? Does no one else want to be here?"

Joni pulled the grate shut, but only just. She clipped it into place. Easy enough to open again, but apparently closed should anyone check. She slid backwards along the steel shaft. "No harm in checking first. See what's going on with him before Joni makes a choice. Why run when Joni might not need to?"

Back over his room. The side of her face pressed against

the cold steel to get the best view of him in his bed. "He's still sleeping. Snoring like a hog. Like the gross pig he is. No sound of anyone else coming. Joni can still do this."

Back at the empty room, Joni freed the hatch again. She threw the bottle of bleach onto the unmade bed, gripped the edge of the maintenance shaft, and lowered herself into the room. The floor beneath her was covered with boxes. Pointing her toes, she hooked the closest upturned box and pulled it towards her.

Joni let go. She went through the bottom of the box with a loud *pop.* A sharp shard of plastic tore into her lower leg, ripping open her shin. She clamped her jaw, her cheeks puffing with her hard exhale. "It's okay." A whisper and no more. She flapped her arms, her sock soaked with blood. "Joni's okay."

Her left leg had escaped injury. Joni pulled her left foot free and stepped beside the box. She pulled out her right leg, avoiding the sharp shard of plastic that had cut into her. Her shredded trousers were damp with her blood. Her right shoe squelched with her steps.

Some spare clothes in one of the boxes, Joni picked up a pair of thick trousers. His trousers? She pinned the end of one trouser leg to the ground with her left foot and pulled. She shook with the effort of opening a small tear on the crotch. She grunted, pulling harder until she tore the trousers in two.

A pool of blood on the steel floor, she wrapped her cut and tied the trouser leg tight. Pins and needles buzzed through her foot. She wiped the box with the other trouser leg and then laid it in the pool of blood to soak up the rest.

"Joni might be wounded, but not so wounded she can't deal with him. Not with such a good opportunity before her. No, she can't pass this up. No matter how bad her pain, she'll give him more." She retrieved her bottle of bleach and hobbled towards the automatic door. *Whoosh!* It opened.

The hallway clear. "He really must be here on his own. By choice? And whose choice? Has he repelled everyone in this place? The vilest of slugs, just sharing the same floor with him has proven too much for everyone else. Joni will do them all a favour. Although, maybe not. Joni wants him to suffer, not die. He doesn't deserve to die. She wants him angry. Furious. Incandescent. Permanently." She hugged her bottle of bleach and nodded. "Yes! Incandescent."

Whoosh! Joni opened his door, but she waited in the hallway. Her rapid pulse throbbed through her wound with a stinging bass drumbeat.

"Nothing." Joni spoke in a whisper. "Is he still really asleep? One step at a time. Softly, softly." She entered his room. The fat hog snored, his mouth open wide. It gave him a double chin. His short, yet scruffy ginger hair protruded from the sides and back of his head. Bald on top. A silly little goatee around his open mouth. A lighter on the bedside table, next to his cigar. Joni picked it up. "Joni should burn off his beard. Turn it redder than red. Set fire to it and him. Melt his skin. No." She shook her head. "Painful, but too quick. He doesn't deserve quick. Never deserved quick. Ever. This is why she came here." She shook the bottle of bleach. A full bottle. She couldn't afford to run out.

He lay on his back. "His eye sockets, two perfect little bowls. Fill 'em up and watch them burn." Joni unscrewed the lid with a shaking hand. The sharp bite of the bleach tingled in her nostrils. "Burn his piggy little eyes out of his fat skull. Would that kill him?" She smiled as she leaned over him and fought to regulate her giddy breaths. Tilting the bottle, a small amount of bleach spilled out and dripped on his bedclothes. "A small amount in his eyes. Maybe one eye? Blind him in one eye and leave the other. Let him see his own reflection. See what she'd done to him. Something to add to the many scars already on his pudgy little body."

Joni's head spun. "Joni needs to be quick and get out of here. Lose too much blood and she might faint." A glass of water on his bedside table. "Maybe Joni needs to be more subtle?" She poured in several drops, the water level in his glass rising, the bleach transparent, but its viscosity made it swirl. "Swirl in his stomach. Swirl until it burns free. Eat him from the inside out. Yes, eat him alive. That'll do nicely. Joni should leave now. Get out of here while … Oh!"

A packet of pills behind his water. Sleeping pills. No wonder he hadn't woken up yet. How often did he use these? "How often will Joni get a chance like this? Dead to the world. Joni can do what she likes, and he won't wake up."

Upending the bottle, she soaked his bed with the thick liquid. The heavy tang burned her nostrils. She ruffled her nose. She could leave, but what would it do to him. "Burn away his sense of smell? Cause his lungs to haemorrhage? He deserves it. No matter what happens, he deserves it all."

Joni left the room. She wore the stink of bleach. The door closed behind her. *Whoosh!*

Back in the empty room with the broken boxes. With her blood on the box and pooled on the floor. The trouser leg had done little to soak it all up. "What if they test the blood? What if they find out it belongs to Joni?" The bed had a mattress and duvet. Pillows with no cases. "All of it will burn. Burn it all. Remove the evidence."

Joni sparked his lighter and held it to the corner of the duvet. The flame licked the off-white fabric. A few seconds later, the fire transferred from her lighter to the duvet. The flame spread, and her eyes widened. "Yes, this is what Joni wanted. Chaos and disorder. He deserves it all."

The burning duvet belched black smoke. It filled the room. Joni stacked the boxes beneath the grate. The one she'd gone through had no lid. Much weaker than the others, so of course she'd gone through it. She pressed down on one of the lidded boxes. "It holds Joni's weight. It supports her just fine."

The higher Joni climbed, the thicker the smoke. Burned plastic mixed with the bleach in her throat. Her oesophagus itched, but she swallowed again while reaching up for the open hatch. "Joni can't have a coughing fit. Not here." She gulped, her voice strained. "How can she burn the evidence and then get caught in the smoke?"

Every gasp tighter than the previous. Stars swam in Joni's vision. She reached up for the hatch. "Burn the evidence of her being there. The evidence and everything else in the place. Burn the whole place down. Burn him."

Joni boosted from the stack of boxes and pulled herself into the maintenance shaft. Her makeshift tower hit the floor with a clattering crash.

She slithered through the tunnel like a snake. Like a predator. "Joni's a snake, and he's the little unsuspecting mouse. Three blind mice. Bleach-blinded mice. She should have burned his eyes."

The smoke caught up with Joni. It filled her lungs. She pulled her shirt up over her mouth and coughed, each bark tearing at her throat. She needed to get out of there.

Back over his room. "But Joni needs to see what she's done to him first." Her throat was sore, the taste of burned plastic on her tongue. Her leg thrummed with the deep cuts. But he still slept. "He has to wake. Joni's done all this, so of course she needs to see his reaction."

Bolts held the grate in place. The same bolts she'd sheered off when she'd kicked the other one open. Joni unscrewed one bolt and dropped it through the bars. It hit the steel floor with a *ting!*

"Stupid." She knocked against the side of her head. "Stupid, stupid, Joni." Smoke filled the surrounding space. Her eyes watered, her lungs tightened. She had no more time.

Joni rolled onto her back and kicked the grate like she had next door. *Crash!* It swung down into his room.

"What?!" He sat up in bed. "What the fuck?"

"That's what Joni needed!" She pulled back, away from the smoke.

He reached across to his bedside table. "Yes." Joni nodded. "Drink the water. Drink it all up. Drink it now and wait for your body to burn. Boil from the inside out. Much better than going blind."

But he opened his drawer. The angle prevented her from seeing what he grabbed.

A burst of bullets tore holes in the maintenance shaft on the other side of the hatch. Small beams of light shone through from the room below.

Joni scooted back, the swish of her fabric against the brushed steel. She had to get out of there. But if she made too much noise, he'd know exactly where to shoot. He'd prove his hunch correct, that someone lived in the shafts. That someone moved through them at least. "He can't know that. He'll send guards up here. This is Joni's playground, not his."

Tracking his footsteps, Joni rolled to the right and leaned against the wall when he shot up, driving more bullet holes into the bottom of the maintenance shaft. She rolled left, onto the sharp pieces of steel from where the bullets had punched through. They dug into her sides.

Another blast of bullets tore holes where she'd just lain.

The smoke thickened. She swallowed again. Every gulp made her throat's itch worse. Cough now and she'd give herself away. She'd show him she used the tunnels. She'd lose her playground. She'd lose access to him.

Clack! He reloaded his gun beneath her. Another magazine. Another chance to kill her.

Joni pushed against the steel base of the shaft. Slowly backwards, away from him. "Be quiet."

Whoop! Whoop! Whoop! The fire alarm went off.

A fist in front of her mouth, Joni coughed into it. Each expulsion shredded her throat.

The man's walkie-talkie hissed. A female voice came through. "This is not a drill. I repeat, this is not a drill."

"Fuck!" the man screamed and shot the shaft again, the bullets only a few feet from Joni, but they went farther away with the man as he left the room. *Whoosh!*

Joni pushed away from the smoke. She stifled her cough, snot shooting from her nose, her stinging eyes streaming. The flat steel aided her retreat. Her escape. He'd turned her into a coward. Left her crawling away on her belly. A spineless worm. And he'd nearly shot her. But he wouldn't get away with it again. Not again. Not ever.

The air clearer the farther she travelled, but Joni still coughed. Burned plastic in her throat and her lungs tight, she coughed again. Each hacking round cleared her airways. She continued to drag herself away. Tears soaked her cheeks. "Next time, Joni will pour bleach into his eyes. Next time, she'll blind him for life. Watch him try to shoot her when he can't see. She'll burn his fucking eyes out. See what happens then. This is what happens when he crosses Joni."

CHAPTER 17

William spun so quickly a string of drool flew from his mouth. The board's whine grew higher in pitch as he turned on the spot. The shouting guards got louder and quieter depending on which way he faced. They closed in, a strobe effect of their progress with his rapid rotations. They passed the catapult, guns raised.

Still no sight of Olga.

The spinning pulled William even farther right. He leaned, his head too heavy. His left leg lifted from the board. He threw out an arm. Dragged at the air like it might re-centre him.

The clacking of another round of bullet fire. William jumped, lost his balance, and flew from the spinning board. He hit a nearby building with a skeleton-jarring *crack!*

William lay on the ground. His world spun. His head throbbed. His shoulder ached from where he'd connected with the steel building. He raised a shaking hand in the guards' direction. "Please, I've done nothing wrong."

Both guards halted, their guns still raised. But through

William's dizzy perspective, they swayed with the rest of their surroundings.

The woman shouted, "Who are you?"

The man freed his walkie-talkie clipped to his grey-uniformed breast.

"Wait!" William said.

The man paused.

The hum of a wheeled board entered the square. Olga rode it like she'd used one for years. She hurtled towards the man with the walkie-talkie, jumped from her board, and slammed into him like a salmon hitting a wet rock. She knocked him on his back, his walkie-talkie skittering away from him.

William stood, but his dizziness threw him back to the ground. He stood again and ran towards the woman, adjusting his diagonal charge to accommodate his loss of balance.

The woman shot just as he fell again, and her bullets streaked over his head.

Intoxicated by his lack of balance, William jumped up and launched himself in her general direction, his arms wide. He tackled her around the waist. They both went down, and she dropped her gun.

The walkie-talkie at her breast hissed static. She grabbed it while William grabbed her gun and levelled it at her. "Drop it!"

The woman froze. Olga also had the man at gunpoint.

"Who are you?" William said. "What are you doing here?"

The woman scowled. "We could say the same to you."

"If you were still holding the guns, you could." William jumped at the sound of bullet fire.

Olga stood over the now dead male guard. She shrugged. "He tried to use his walkie-talkie."

The woman snapped the walkie-talkie to her mouth.

William pulled her gun's trigger. A burst of five or six bullets. Each one sank into her face, ripping it to shreds. The destruction buried what she'd once looked like. Now a limp and mutilated corpse. Blood pooled beneath her.

Olga sneered. Her eyes glazed as she stared down at the male guard. "We saw what they did to that man. They deserve this."

"Hopefully we stopped them alerting anyone to our presence. Hopefully we have a minute." William pointed his gun at his wheeled board. "Can you teach me how to ride that thing?"

Olga nodded. "It's all about weight distribution." She stepped onto her board with one foot. "It won't move until you have both feet on it." She stepped on with the other. "If you want it to go forward, you press down with your toes." She zipped forwards. "To go back, you rest on your heels." She shot backwards. "If you want it to turn, you put pressure on either side of the board." She spun a full circle, smiled, and winked at him. "But you've already learned that move, eh?" Her smile fell. They were in the square with a fired catapult and three dead bodies. "We should leave."

William stepped onto the board. One foot first. When he stepped on with his second, he leaned forward just a little, and the board slowly rolled. He put pressure on his left foot, and the board turned. He stopped the spin with his right.

"Ready?" Olga said.

"I think so?"

"Come on, then." She led the way back out onto the road, and William followed. She went slowly, allowing him to keep up.

"You know," William said, "I might get used to this. I—"

"Shh!" Olga stopped.

William didn't. Couldn't. He rolled past her. "What?"

"Hear that?"

"Wha … oh!"

Clack-clack! Clack-clack! Clack-clack! "Shit!" William said. "Dogs!"

"And drones. The guards might not have called in what just happened, but they're still coming this way."

"They must have seen the catapulted bits."

"I'd say so." Olga flicked her head to show the way. "Come on, let's get out of here." She shot off.

William had only just learned how to stand on the thing, but he had no more time to take it slowly. He leaned forward and took off after her.

CHAPTER 18

Gracie paced in their cell, every step snapping through her, running all the way up her body and jogging her aching, swollen face. Could she take another beating? Could she take her own advice again? "Whatever's going to happen to us, she's just made it worse."

Matilda rolled her eyes, shook her head, and looked out across the plaza. At the people on the perimeter. Silent predators. Ravenous carnivores. They watched on. They bided their time.

"She's playing into their hands." Gracie threw her arms away from her body. "She's doing exactly what they want. She's playing their game, and we're all going to pay the price. If only you'd just—"

"Jeez!" Matilda stepped towards Gracie, stamping her foot. Her brow locked in a scowl. "Do you *ever* shut up?"

Gracie balled her fists and pulled her shoulders back. "*What* did you say?"

The people in the surrounding cages stirred. Many of them leaned against their bars. They might not understand one another, but some things were universal. Like an argument between two people. Were they seeing a weakness in the three strangers' defence? Something to exploit?

"You've made your point." Matilda either didn't notice the change in atmosphere outside their cage, or she didn't care. "I get it. You don't think we should fight. Going on about it doesn't make the point any more effective. Quite the opposite, in fact. You chose not to fight. I didn't. Deal with it."

"That's the problem."

"What is?"

"You fought, and now we all have to face the consequences."

"If you're so sure about my actions being wrong and yours being right, tell me what's going to happen now I've fought back?"

"They're going to pull us out for more fights."

"And you can prove they weren't going to do that anyway?"

"They'll beat the shit out of us."

Matilda stepped back to make a point of looking Gracie up and down.

"Look." Gracie glanced at Hawk, who turned away from her attention like a scolded child. Not his argument. "Whatever happens, it won't be good."

"Unlike the paradise we had waiting for us?"

"You don't know these people."

"Neither do you."

Gracie rested her hands on her hips and tried to breathe in through her clogged and swollen nose.

"You know the people from the community near Dout. The people with whom you were at war. The people who *had* to hate you because their lives *literally* depended on it. You—"

"Oh, look." Gracie nodded across the square. "Here's another one. Already."

The large woman with the wiry mousy brown hair

entered the plaza from the opposite side. Like before, the silent prisoners recoiled at her proximity. If that didn't convince Matilda they needed to fear this woman, then what would? "She's already back. Thanks to you."

Matilda showed Gracie her right palm. "Stop it! I made the choice I made. Deal with it."

Gracie chewed the inside of her mouth and winced from the sharp sting electrifying the right side of her face. She let her jaw hang loose.

Like before, the thickset woman had guards. Six this time. They were larger than her, but none were meaner. She stomped across the square, her brow locked, her massive hands balled into fists. A slight girl no older than Matilda walked behind her. Another skinny fighter. Another part of their elaborate plan to lure them into a false sense of security before they turned all the other prisoners on them. Before they made them pay for who they were and what they'd done to these kids.

The bulky woman pointed at Hawk, and Gracie spoke from the side of her mouth. "Look how quickly they've come back for another fight, *thanks* to Matilda. They won't stop until they've broken us."

"Look," Matilda said, "I can't tell you what to do—"

Thunk! The woman unlocked the cage and pulled the door wide, stepping aside to let Hawk out.

"But," Matilda went on, "I can make my own choices. If I'm forced into a fight with someone where the choice is to fight back or to take a kicking, I'm going to fight back."

"Who's that?" Gracie nodded at where the woman and her crew had entered. Another woman. She had bright pink hair. Much leaner than the lump who'd unlocked their cage, but built like a warrior. She wore a white vest, her bulging arms on display. Her tight black trousers revealed every muscle in her powerful legs. She had broad shoulders. Covered in scars, she wore a deep scowl. She stood with her legs shoulder width apart and had her arms folded across her chest. She watched Hawk.

"I'm not sure." Matilda shook her head. "And how does she get her hair that colour?"

"Really?"

Matilda shrugged.

Gracie spoke from the side of her mouth. "Hawk, don't fight back."

Hawk stood in front of the slight girl, the crusty bandage still wrapped around his neck. If he took too much of a kicking, his wounds would tear open again. Could Gracie really ask him to hold back? Everyone watched on: the silent prisoners, the nasty woman who organised the fight, the pink-haired, scowling warrior.

"Hawk, it's a trap."

"Maybe it's not," Matilda said. "Maybe we need to let Hawk decide his actions."

The lead woman stood between Hawk and the girl like she had between Matilda and the boy. She raised her thick arm, elicited a nod from Hawk and his opponent, and cut the air between them with a full-bodied swipe.

Hawk ran at the girl, and Gracie slumped where she stood. Hadn't he seen the woman who had just walked into the place? "Haw—"

Crack! He caught the girl with his first shot.

The girl stumbled and fell on her arse.

The warrior with the pink hair bristled. She straightened her back and swayed from side to side.

Standing over her, panting, Hawk's face twisted as if pained. He didn't want this like Gracie hadn't wanted it.

"Yeargh!" The girl propelled herself from the ground, her

arms spread wide. She went to tackle Hawk around the waist.

Crack! Hawk kneed her in the face. Straight in her nose.

The girl fell flat.

"Shit!" Gracie said.

"*You* might want him to abstain from fighting," Matilda said, "but by doing that, you're asking him to take a kicking. I've not given up on getting out of here, and I want to make sure I'm as strong as I can be to seize the opportunity when it comes. Why shouldn't Hawk be allowed to do the same?"

Gracie opened her mouth to reply, but she had no words.

A cornered dog, Hawk turned from the woman leading the fights to her guards. Which one would attack him next? If he went down, he'd go down fighting. And he might have to. He'd given them what they wanted. It would only get worse for him now.

The woman with the mousy brown hair approached him. She grabbed his arm and dragged him back towards the cage.

Thunk! One of the large woman's guards unlocked the cage, and the woman shoved Hawk inside. The pink-haired warrior remained on the other side of the square. She watched on for a few more seconds before walking away. They'd not seen the last of her.

As Hawk passed Gracie, he mumbled to the ground, "I'm sorry, but I agree with Matilda. If my choice is to fight or take a beating, I'll choose to fight every time."

Gracie shrugged. Neither he nor Matilda trusted her judgement. She knew these people. She knew what they were like. They'd see. But maybe it made no difference whether they fought. They were prisoners. These people would do what they pleased with them anyway.

The sadist and her team of bodyguards left via the same exit as the pink-haired woman. The prisoners' sunken eyes tracked them before they returned their attention to Gracie, Hawk, and Matilda.

"Wha—!" Matilda jumped away from the cage door.

A man stood beside them. Slight, he had tanned skin, wore robes, and had a shaved head that glistened under the sun's weak glare. The first stranger in this place who didn't look like he wanted to kill them. Should they fear him the most? He held one of the brown bars towards Matilda, poking it through the cage like feeding an animal.

"Matilda, don—"

Matilda took the bar and bit into it. She held it towards Gracie, but the man said something they didn't understand and produced another two bars. One for Gracie and one for Hawk.

Hawk would follow Matilda off a cliff. He went straight to the man, took the bar, and smiled as he bit into it. Had they forgotten they were prisoners? That their lives weren't their own.

The man said words Gracie didn't understand and shoved the bar towards her. His soft brown eyes spoke of a gentle soul. But she knew these people. They'd used him because of his appearance. He'd get them to lower their guard before they screwed them over.

The other prisoners shouted at the man. His calm expression remained unchanged. He shoved the bar in Gracie's direction again.

But Gracie shook her head. She pointed two fingers down her throat, miming that she might get sick from it. How did she know what it contained?

The man broke the bar into chunks and held them towards her. He pointed at the bar, his finger hovering over the pieces. Gracie indicated her lump of choice, which he popped into his mouth, chewed up, and swallowed. He stuck his tongue out to show her it had all gone and shoved the broken pieces towards her again.

Gracie approached the man with slow steps. She took the remains of the broken bar and slipped a chunk into her mouth. The sweet relief spread across her tongue. She shrugged. “If we’re going to die anyway …” She placed another chunk on her tongue.

CHAPTER 19

William's stomach turned faster than his board's wheels. He teetered on the edge of his balance, leaning into the strange whining vehicle's acceleration. Already at full speed, if he leaned any farther forward, he'd face-plant into the rough concrete ground and probably loose half his features to the sandpaper surface. The gun he'd stolen from the guard hung across his front from its leather strap. Head down against the chilly wind, tears streaked across his temples.

Beside him, Olga, the personification of core strength, leaned into her rapid progress as if she could hold her pose for days. Other than her hard squint because of the head-wind, she stood at ease.

Entrances to roads and alleys broke up the monotony of the tall walls. Industrial plazas and residential squares. A grey blur of high steel, broken by the *thwip* of changing acoustics because of each opening.

William shouted over the hum of their tyres and their whining engines. "You're sure you've never done this before?"

At full speed, yet Olga turned William's way and smiled. "I've come from the same world as you."

"What does that mean?"

"When would I have had the chance to do this?"

They flew towards another white line, with the glass light coverings on either side atop the thick steel walls. The lights were off. The hum of rubber against rough concrete gave way to a momentary *slap* of them passing over the two-foot-wide bar of thick paint.

The road stretched away for miles. Olga checked behind. If William even thought about doing anything other than looking where they were going, he'd do a ninety-degree turn into one of the massive walls. And unstoppable force versus an immovable object. His weak organic form would be the thing that yielded.

"We need to get off this road soon." Olga checked behind again. "We're vulnerable out here."

Another white line, the lights on either side burst to life and flashed red. William gasped. "What does that mean?"

"Dunno, but I'm sure it's not good."

Several more lines ahead. All of them marked by flashing red lights.

"Hear that?" Olga said.

A hum like their own. A whine like that coming from the small motors driving their wheeled boards. Like their own, but deeper. Something far more powerful. They carried more weight. More force.

"Follow me." Olga leaned back on her board and slowed.

William decelerated and thrust his arms out to his sides to maintain his balance. He followed his short friend into an industrial section. Several large buildings like the last one they'd entered, but no catapult this time. And no armed guards. Yet.

The humming closed in on them. A deep rumble of

several sets of tyres. *Whomp!* One shot past. *Whomp!* And then another. "Tanks."

"Like the ones we saw at the wall," Olga said.

As the humming grew distant, William forced his cheeks out with his exhale. "That was lucky."

Olga raised her eyebrows. "We have to do better at hiding from now on. That road isn't the one."

"I agre—"

Thunk! A brick of heavy steel about the size of William's wheeled board landed close to them. It sent a stinging spray of chipped concrete against his shins, skittered across the ground, and slammed into the steel wall beside them.

Thunk! Another lump. William raised his hands to shield his face from the concrete chips.

A group of about ten people emerged from one hut. All of them held metal bricks.

"Come on!" Olga spun around and shot back out into the road.

Thunk! William twitched when another lump landed close to him. His jolt sent the board forwards, and he nearly fell off the back. Maybe he didn't have as much control as he first thought. He tested his movement with a gentle press of his toes.

Thunk! The next lump landed closer than the last.

William pressed hard and spun on the spot. His body leaned with the g-force of his turn. He caught it by pressing with his other foot. Facing the road, he leaned forward and shot from the square.

Clang! One final lump skittered into the wall beside him as he drove back out onto the wider road.

The hum of tyres against concrete.

The long road stretched away from them for miles.

The wind flapped in William's ears.

Clack-clack!

"Shit! Dogs!"

"Follow me." Olga took the next right.

Another plaza, this one filled with small residential huts. They slowed just enough to navigate the weaving path through the tight walkways and alleys. The residents shouted at them as they passed.

Doors behind them slammed shut. A domino effect racing towards them from the edge of the plaza. Where William and Olga had drawn people from their homes, the hum of drones and *clack-clack* of dogs pushed them back in again. The slamming doors overtook them. Those ahead withdrew and hid before they could abuse the passing pair.

William glanced behind, wobbled, and settled back into the motion of the board. He'd finally found the nuance in the subtle pressure required to control the thing. A few feet behind Olga, he weaved left and right. He pulled his arms in when he passed through some of the tighter alleys between the one-storey buildings. Any tighter and they'd have to go on foot. "You think they can track us?" He pointed at his feet. "You think they can track these things?"

Olga shook her head. "Those tanks would have found us if they could. But I think the red lights are for us. I think the place is on high alert after our run-in with those guards. Hopefully, if we hide, we can avoid them."

"So where do we hid—oh!"

Olga's guiding finger answered him. A building similar in height to those surrounding it, but it only had three walls and an open front. A shed of sorts. A shelter. A stable. Not that he'd seen any animals in this place. They closed in on it.

The stable contained boxes and trolleys that must have been used to move things around. Nothing motorised or powered here.

William wriggled his nose to rid it of the funk of dirt. But the stench formed as much a part of this place as the steel walls, concrete ground, and hessian hanging across the back. "You think this is the best place to hide?"

Now they'd stopped, the drones' hum and the dogs' *clack-clack* spoke of their pursuers' proximity. "No." Olga shook her head. "But it's the best we have."

William's abs ached, but he remained balanced on his board. A quick getaway should they need it. Did they have the speed to outrun the dogs and drones? To avoid bullets and flames? He slowed his rampaging heart by breathing in through his nose and out through his mouth. Slow and steady. Rhythmic. In and out. In and out.

Clack-clack! Clack-clack! The dogs drew closer, and they brought the hum of their hovering friends.

"Do you thi—" Darkness smothered William. The brown hessian came to life and swamped him. A hand wrapped around the bottom half of his face, gagging him. The reek of dirt and sweat filled his nostrils.

William's eyes adjusted to the dark. They were in a pit hidden behind the sheet, the sack and rest of the stable in front of them. The hessian formed a curtain between them and the outside world. A boy about William's age held Olga like the person held him. Olga's eyes were wide, but not as wide as those of the twenty or so dirty faces of the others in the pit. From children to teenagers, some of them looked as young as five or six.

William twisted against the person's restraint, but they tightened their grip. They shot a sharp, "Shh!" into his ear.

The drones and dogs had slowed outside. *Clack ... clack! Clack ... clack!* They were getting closer.

Some kids whimpered and gasped. The older kids pulled them in and hugged them to keep them quiet.

The person who'd grabbed William let him go. William spun, his fists raised, but the boy, about his age, stood with a finger pressed to his lips. He pointed at the sack curtain between them and death.

William filled his lungs with the place's dirty stench. He slowly let his breath go and nodded.

The person holding Olga let her go, too. They passed William and Olga and moved closer to the hessian sheet.

William and Olga followed. The porous fabric and the light outside afforded them a blurred view of the world beyond.

Several of the children whispered and cried. One boy beside William silenced them with a hard scowl. Shut up or else!

William snapped taut and clapped a hand across his own mouth to stifle his reaction.

A drone entered first. A deep hum and a bright light on top. It dazzled William, the glare burning his eyes. He gripped the guard's gun, but the boy beside him pushed it down and shook his head.

Clack ... clack! Clack ... clack! A dog entered with slow and deliberate steps.

William trembled. They were currently standing in the perfect roasting pit, and they only had a thin sheet of flammable fabric as their protection.

The dog moved closer, following the drone. Both of them just a few feet from the sack. The dog had a weaker strip of lights across its brow, but its glow added to the drone's glare. Between them, they lit up the shed. They revealed the useless items in the place. The dog's light reflected off a glass circle attached to the bottom of the drone. A lens. The drone's light showed the dog had one in its mouth. They both carried cameras. Someone was watching. But who?

CHAPTER 20

"Joni's going to give him hell. And he'll deserve every second of the torture. She'll make him sob and apologise for everything he's ever done. He deserves it all. She'll give him hell. Take him to hell. Bring hell to him. Hell's bells. All's well that ends well. But it won't." She shook her head. "It won't end well for him. No chance. Whatever it takes, Joni will make sure he gets what's been coming to him for a long time." She clasped her hands in front of her chest and grinned. "A long, long time."

Bathed in the glow of twenty screens. Most of the footage moving, feeding back to her as they roamed the place. A dog's-eye view. A drone's-eye view. All moving save for the screen in the centre. Still knocked, it focused on the wall by the gates. No use to anyone.

She'd left him hours ago, but the taste of burned plastic remained fused to the back of her throat. Every gulp sore and laced with the chemical flavour of burned bedding. "Next time it will be burning flesh. Joni will make him scream.

"Huh?" Joni leaned closer to the screen in the top right-hand corner. A drone's-eye view of the plaza. One of many. One of hundreds. A catapult. Two fallen guards. "Dead? Is someone killing guards? What happened to those who killed them? They will be punished. They'll regret what they've done. On the run. No fun. No." She shook her head so hard drool flew from her mouth onto several screens. "No fun."

"I'm hungry!"

Joni spun right to face the steel door. Locked. Always locked. The little chick didn't get to choose when he left. She knew what was best for him and when. He needed to trust that. She laughed. "He has to trust that. Mama Bird knows best."

"I'm hungry!"

"How can you be hungry again?"

His whining voice, muffled by the steel door, shot back at her. "I'm hungry."

It turned her spine like a corkscrew. "Joni knows you're hungry. We're all hungry. That's what this world is. What, do you think Joni's only here to feed you? To make sure you—"

"I'm hungry."

"Arghhhhhh!" Joni clapped her hands to the sides of her head and pressed hard. "Joni hears you." Spittle sprayed from her mouth. "You're hungry. But what if Joni's busy? What if Joni has things she needs to do? What if Joni needs to give herself time first? What then?"

"I'm hungry."

Joni rocked in her seat. Towards the screens and back. Towards the screens and back. She shook her head. Again and again and again.

"I'm hungry."

Jumping to her feet, Joni pointed at the locked door. "Joni knows what to do to shut him up. To fuck him up. You asked for Joni, and now she's coming. You'd best be steady, ready. Are you ready, Eddie?"

Thunk! Joni unlocked the door. A chunk of deer meat in her right hand, she pulled it open with her left. The hinges cackled. They knew her plans.

"And there he is." The little chick lay strapped to the trolley. Helpless. Flightless. "Not so hungry now, are you? Careful what you ask for, little chick. But you wanted Joni. Well, here she is. Don't be shy now."

Joni leaned over him. He kept his eyes closed. Kept playing games with her. Dried deer meat clung to his lips from where she'd last fed him. Some of it stuck to his teeth. Joni tilted her head to one side. "How hungry are you? You've not eaten your last meal." She pressed a dirty finger against his face, squashing his cheek. Dried meat spilled from his mouth like maggots from a foetid wound.

"Nothing?" With only the echo of her own voice for company, Joni paused. "Really? You're still pretending to be knocked out? You won't shut up when Joni's resting. Now she's in here, you play dead. What's the time, Mr. Wolf? How close does Joni need to get before it's dinner time? What, you think Joni will release the straps, little chick? Little chick, little pig, little tic, little sprig." Joni's echo joined in with her tittering laugh. Her voice bounced off the hard stone walls. They glistened with damp like everything in this place. "Damp cramp ramp."

Joni bit a chunk of deer meat from the lump she'd taken from him. "And she's going to take more. So much more. The less he has, the better. Joni will take it all. You won't complain about being hungry soon, little chick. Joni will have it all. Joni will have more than you can eat."

The meat now considerably drier than when she'd first taken it, chewing it dragged the saliva from Joni's mouth. "Like eating cardboard. But Joni can chew. Make it nice and juicy for the little chick. That's what mamas do best, right?

He's hungry. The least Joni can do is give him a good meal. He is her guest, after all. Her little chick."

Her jaw ached, but the little chick needed to be cared for. Joni pulled a pinch of meat from her mouth and rolled it into a ball. A pellet. She pressed it against his face, shoved it against his teeth. Under his lips like before. "Stuff it in. Save it for later. Play dead all you like. Just know that Joni looks out for you."

Some of the tension left Joni's wiry frame. "That's better now, isn't it, little chick? Joni wants to destroy, but she can care too. She can look after people like you. Help you. Guide you. Raise you. Praise you."

His lips and cheeks were filled with deer meat. Joni stroked his clammy forehead. "It's there for you when you're ready. No more moaning, yeah? Joni nearly got cross, and you don't want to make Mama Bird cross now, do you?"

At the door, the hinges cackled again when Joni pulled it wide.

"I'm hungry."

She spun around.

He remained still, like he hadn't moved, his cheeks swollen with deer meat.

Joni wagged a finger at him. "Ah! Hilarious, little chick."

Crash! She pulled the door shut behind her. *Thunk!* She turned the key in the lock.

Her back against the cold steel door, Joni addressed the damp ceiling. "Why is Joni letting him get to her? Why does she obsess over him? She's a mama now. She has baby chicks to feed. Why does she waste her time thinking about him? There are bandages to be changed and beaks to be stuffed."

While shaking her head, Joni walked towards the other locked door. "Bandages to be changed. Joni's wasted too much time on him. She's spent years tormenting him. But it needs to end. He needs to end. Goodbye, friend." She screwed up her face. "Not friend. Never friend. Bell end. She needs to end him. She needs to fulfil her true purpose. She can do that and be a mama to her chicks."

Thunk! Joni unlocked the next door and shoved it wide. "Mama Bird's here to change your bandages." This one still hadn't woken. Still strapped to the bed. He'd lost a lot of blood. Would he ever wake? "Nature's cruel. Not all the chicks survive. But Mama Bird can win. She can beat nature, *and* she can beat him. She can beat them all."

CHAPTER 21

The fire's small flames hypnotised Gracie. She lost focus and fell into a rhythm with their mesmerising sway. Everything ached. Her muscles, skin, and heart. Fatigue, swelling, remorse. She should have done more in Dout. She should have told them about Max's error.

The gong of the man's steel pan broke her from her daze. Over a small fire, he dropped in a thin slice of pink meat. It hissed and spat. It cooked in seconds, shrinking and curling in the heat. A boy helped the man. About Artan's age, he had a similar physique. Strong. Fit. The man barked orders, and the boy obeyed, wrapping the meat in bread and passing the food through the bars to first Matilda and then Hawk.

Matilda's eyes widened when she bit into the roll. She spoke with her mouth full. "Oh. My. This is good!"

It might be good, but what if there was something wrong with it? Poisoned? Drugged? Why were they taking such good care of their prisoners? What did they have planned?

A pale birthmark covered half the boy's face. The rest of his visible skin was as dark as the man's cooking for them. They could well be kin. The boy's smile and bright eyes disarmed Gracie. His confidence spoke of someone wise beyond his years. Maybe his words did too, but trying to ascertain the meaning of their strange language had proven to be futile in the past, so why try now? She took the food, and in the face of his clear joy at giving it to her, she took a bite.

"Wow!" The salty meat mixed with the melted butter. Gracie covered her mouth while she spoke. "You were right, Matilda. This *is* good!"

They might have spoken an unfamiliar language, but the boy understood Gracie's enjoyment. The man had the same beaming grin as he retrieved a small glass jar from his basket. He passed it to the boy, who passed it to Gracie. It reeked of antiseptic. The man mimed poking two fingers into the pot and spreading it across his face. He pointed at Gracie. He dragged his fingers along his neck and then pointed at Hawk.

Gracie scooped out some of the cream and winced when she touched her hot and swollen skin. Both man and boy grinned and nodded, so she added more, the cream leaving a thick and greasy layer on her face.

Although Gracie offered the tub to Hawk, he simply stared at it. "You'll take their food, but not their ointment?"

Matilda's gentle words encouraged Gracie to lower the pot. "It's like the stuff from Grandfather Jacks' palace."

Hawk's eyes glazed, and he sighed. He held his hand towards Gracie. "Sorry." He stared at the ground and took the pot. "It forced me back to a place I didn't plan on revisiting today."

"No, I'm sorry. I should have thought."

Matilda rested a hand on the back of Gracie's forearm. "You weren't to know. When I was injured, Hawk got something similar for me. Grandfather Jacks used to use it on their wounds."

Hawk peeled the fabric from his neck with shaking

hands, revealing both his scars from the lacerations and healing wounds from his recent cuts.

Gracie took the pot back from Hawk. "Look up."

He did as instructed, stretching his neck to give Gracie easier access to his wound. She applied a layer of the thick cream, Hawk wincing and twitching at her contact. "I'm sorry they did this to you. I should have fought back."

"You weren't to know. We all d—"

The prisoners around the plaza's perimeter came to life. They banged against their cages' bars with shoes and small rocks. They howled and whistled. The woman with the pink hair entered and strolled with the ease of someone used to this kind of ovation. She brought an entourage of ten to fifteen people. Men, women, and young fighters. The large woman who'd arranged all the other fights walked among them.

Hawk wrapped the fabric around his neck again and pressed against the place where Gracie had applied the ointment. "Why didn't she get this welcome last time?"

"She's come here to fight." Gracie's stomach sank, and her face throbbed from where she'd applied the cream. "I'll fight her."

"You really think that's what she's here for?" Matilda said.

"Look at her. If that's not someone ready for combat, I don't know what is. And it's my turn."

Now led by the large woman with the mousy brown hair, the warrior and her entourage approached Gracie, Matilda, and Hawk's cage. The man who'd cooked for them stepped away and dragged his son with him.

Thunk! The large woman opened the door and pointed at Matilda.

"No!" Gracie stood up and jabbed her chest with her thumb. "I'm fighting. It's my turn."

The woman pointed at Matilda again.

When Matilda stepped forwards, Gracie pulled her back and pointed at herself. She spoke louder, as if shouting would somehow make the woman better understand. "I'm fighting. Me, not her."

The woman's scowl seemed to be a permanent fixture. She shook her head at Gracie and pointed to Matilda. Several of the men and women in the entourage bristled. If they had to use force …

"It's fine." Matilda rested a hand on Gracie's arm. She slipped past and followed the woman out of the cage. "They want me to fight. Your injuries need more time to heal."

"I'm sorry, Matilda. I didn't know it would come to this."

Just before she left the cage, Matilda smiled. "Honestly, it's fine. None of us knew what was coming."

The prisoners grew more raucous at Matilda's exit. She rolled her shoulders and snapped her head from side to side. No doubt this time. She'd fight back.

While those around them whipped into a frenzy, Gracie chewed on her bottom lip and sidled closer to Hawk. "I didn't know it would come to this."

"None of us did."

The large woman stood between Matilda and the pink-haired lady like she'd stood between every other fighting pair.

Covered in scars, her arms as thick as Gracie's thighs, the pink-haired lady raised her guard and bounced on her toes. "She's going to destroy Matilda."

"Have faith," Hawk said.

"I lost that a long time ago."

Hawk snorted a laugh. "Me too. But Matilda's a warrior."

The large woman dropped her arm.

The lady with the pink hair lunged forwards and caught Matilda clean on the chin. *Crack!*

Matilda stumbled back, held her jaw as if checking it still

fitted, and jumped aside when the pink-haired lady charged her again.

On her next charge, Matilda drove the woman back with a straight jab to her nose.

The prisoners hissed with their collective dragging of air through clenched teeth.

Giddy with adrenaline that balled as nausea in her gut, Gracie shook her head. "She shouldn't have done that."

"I dunno." Hawk shrugged. "Maybe the woman wants a fight."

Dodging the woman's next attack, Matilda followed up with another blow to the face and one to the woman's stomach. The second lifted the woman from the ground.

The pink-haired fighter stumbled. Her mouth wide, she fought for breath. Matilda went in for another attack, but the woman caught her with an uppercut to the chin.

Matilda's eyes glazed. Her legs wobbled.

The pink-haired woman charged.

Matilda quickened her stumbling retreat as if she could outrun her attacker.

But the woman sped up. She spread her arms wide to tackle Matilda around the waist.

Matilda's focus returned.

Gracie's jaw fell. "She was pretending."

Matilda stepped aside, grabbed the woman's shirt, and used her momentum against her. She lifted her from the ground and launched her, slamming her back into the cage she'd retreated towards.

The pink-haired lady hit the ground and brayed like a donkey. Her entourage closed in on Matilda, who raised her arms in surrender.

The downed fighter shouted at them through her barking gasps. She stood on wobbly legs.

"What's she doing?" Hawk said.

"She's telling them to leave Matilda alone."

Matilda backed away. She dropped into a defensive crouch and raised her fists. She lowered her guard when the pink-haired woman pressed the palms of her hands together as if in prayer and bowed.

Frowning hard, Matilda bowed back.

Matilda might have lowered her guard, but she kept her fists balled. Two of the woman's entourage led her back to the cage. She threw glances at the woman she'd fought. Would she attack her from behind?

Thunk! One man opened the cage, and the other pulled the door wide.

Matilda entered.

"What was that about?" Gracie said.

Matilda shrugged. "Who knows?"

"It's messed up, that's what it is. I'm sorry you had to fight instead of me."

"It's fine, Gracie, honestly."

Gracie's voice grew louder with every word. "I don't know why these people are making us fight. Why they're playing with us. Actually, why wouldn't they? They hate us. Beat us up in front of the prisoners. Use us as a cautionary tale. This is what we can do to people. I wonder when they'll drag us out and ceremoniously cut our throats."

Clack-clack! Clack-clack! Dogs' footsteps. The hum of drones accompanied them.

The man who'd cooked for them shoved his son into the cage with Gracie and the others. He slammed the door shut. He pressed a button on the side. *Whoosh!* Steel panels shot up from the ground to the cage's roof. The top closed off too, throwing Gracie and the others into utter darkness.

"What's going on?" Hawk said.

Gracie's lungs tightened. "What are they doing?"

Even through the steel panels, the *clack-clack* of the dogs called to them. Gracie raised her voice. "What's going on?"

"Shh!" the boy with the birthmark said.

"Don't you *shh* me!" Gracie spoke to the darkness. Had she been able to locate the boy, she might have swung for him.

A hand clamped across Gracie's mouth. The boy had snuck up behind her. He leaned so close to her ear, the skin at the base of her back tingled. A gentle delivery this time. "Shh!"

Like she had a choice. One sharp tug and he'd snap her neck.

CHAPTER 22

"Shh!" A firm grip locked onto William's bicep and pulled him back. Again! Olga beside him, he spoke beneath his breath. "I'm tiring of this. At what point do we fight our way out of here?"

The person gripped harder and fired yet another burst of air into his ear. "Shh!"

Olga's lips tightened. She raised her eyebrows. "It's not gotten violent."

"Yet." Red digits glowed on the top of William's gun. Thirty-two. Olga's read thirty-one. Maybe they were the squad numbers of the guards they'd killed? He tilted his weapon to get Olga's attention. "But it could."

Olga's eyes pinched at the sides. She shook her head ever so slightly. And maybe she had a point. They were stuck in a hole in the ground with mostly kids. The air reeked of their anxiety. Anxiety, flatulence, and sweat.

Bright light flooded the place. The glare dazzled William, but it also revealed the pit. A slanted hole dug into the ground. The walls made from crumbling earth, no doubt crawling with worms. The surrounding children recoiled from the light, some of them moaning at the sudden change. They were nocturnal, pathetic creatures. Olga was right, there was no need for violence against them.

Propelled forwards by a powerful hand in his back, William stumbled for several steps and landed on his knees on the rough concrete.

Olga yelped when she fell beside him. She bit down on her bottom lip and breathed through her nose.

The two larger boys who'd held them the entire time threw out their wheeled boards and withdrew, pulling the sheet back across as quickly as they'd ripped it open. The stable returned to being a stable. Old boxes, a hessian sheet, a cart for moving heavier items. Nothing to see here. Of course they watched them through the porous fabric, but they'd let them go now the dogs and drones had moved on. William raised an eyebrow. "I'm guessing they think it's safe for us to leave?"

"And why didn't they kill us?"

"You're complaining?"

"Not at all. Just curious." Olga rolled her shoulders and rubbed her eyes.

William's own burned while they readjusted to the daylight. "I guess, in that moment, we shared an enemy. And I'm guessing they held us in here long enough to make sure we could leave without blowing both ours and their cover."

"But why were they hiding when no one else was? And why all kids?"

"There are many things about this place that baffle me, and I'm not sure I care enough to find out. Not until we're reunited with Matilda and the others." William stepped onto his board. He applied light pressure with his toes and edged towards the shed's exit.

Even brighter outside, Olga pulled level with William. "I still think we should head to the building in the centre."

"Again?"

"I think it's the best plan."

"You've said. Countless times."

"That's because you're not listening."

"I am listening."

"Then you're not hearing."

William rubbed his still sore eyes. "Maybe you're the one not hearing. How many times do I have to say it? I'm not giving up on Matilda like you—"

"Like I what?" Olga stopped, her cheeks flushed red. "Like I what? Gave up on Max? Is that what you were going to say?" She pointed at William. "I wasn't the one who left and then came back. I wasn't the one who abandoned him. That was all you. Sure, I failed to see what he truly needed, but I *never* gave up on him. Don't you dare …" She clenched her jaw against her quivering bottom lip. Her voice broke. "I *never* gave up on him. Not for a second."

CHAPTER 23

"What the hell is this place?" William stopped his wheeled board, and Olga halted beside him. The first thing he'd said to her since the Max comment hours ago. The roads and paths had all been the same save for their varying width. Miles of tall steel walls. Miles of rough concrete roads. Their travels punctuated by plazas and squares. Industrial and social spots. Residential. All unremarkable. Different in appearance, but uniform in their dreariness. The onset of night had slowed them down. With the moon to guide them, they moved at half their daytime speed. Even slower on the narrower streets.

A plaza like many before it. They hung back near the main entrance. Unlike those they'd already passed, this one had cages around its perimeter, and spotlights lit up the centre of the square. A woman with pink hair battled a wiry man under the glow of the lights. Under the silent threat of the static sentry guns. She took a couple of shots before returning a hammer blow to his chin. She followed up with a chop to his throat.

The man rolled on the ground, clutching his neck. William said, "Olga? Any ideas?"

"I *dunno* what this place is. I would have said if I'd known. Why are you asking me? What's my opinion worth?"

"Don't be like that."

"You're a dick, you know that?"

"I know. I shouldn't have said what I did. I'm sorry. And I was wrong. *We* failed Max, not you. We put the pressure on both of you to leave before he was ready. Had we not done that, things would be a lot different."

The muscles along the side of Olga's jaw tensed and relaxed. Her bottom lip quivered again. She remained fixed on the square. "I wanna know how she got her hair that colour."

William half-smiled as the woman knocked another man to the ground. One punch and he went down. "I wanna know where she learned to punch like that."

Malnourished prisoners occupied cages around the plaza's perimeter. Many of them clung to the bars like the steel rods were the only things keeping them standing. They watched the fights through wide eyes in their gaunt faces. One container sat amongst the steel cages. It had opaque sides and roof. "What do you think's in there?"

Olga shrugged. "Supplies?"

"You think it's worth robbing?"

"You already know what I think."

"We should head to the guards' block?"

Olga's face remained blank.

William sighed. His shoulders sank with his exhale. "I think we should go with your plan."

"So you want to listen to me now?"

"Would you like me to apologise again? I was wrong. I'm sorry. You were right. We could end up searching this place for days and get no closer to finding the others. They're more than capable of looking after themselves. They can find their own way to the guards' block."

Olga dragged in air through her clenched teeth when the pink-haired lady dropped another prisoner. "You know what, even if someone could tell me, I'm not sure I want to know what that woman's doing and why." She reversed her wheeled board, backing away from the square. "There's too much shit going on in this place. I don't want any part of it. Come on, let's go. I think we should find somewhere to rest. We'll make much better progress when it's light."

The dirty square with the dirty prisoners and the pink-haired lady posed an interesting question, but William agreed; the less they knew, the better. Get to the guards' block and meet up with the others. Matilda, Hawk, and Gracie were big enough and brave enough to look out for themselves. The feeling in his gut about Matilda being in trouble was fuelled by anxiety, not intuition. Of course he'd worry about her until he saw her again, but he needed to be sensible. He needed to listen to Olga. And for all he knew, they were already there waiting for them. His delaying might be the thing putting them at risk by forcing them to stay in a dangerous area. He spun on the spot and took off after his friend. Tonight they'd rest. Tomorrow they'd get to the guards' block and find their friends.

CHAPTER 24

Thunk! The steel shutters fell, and Gracie yelped. She rolled away from them on instinct, whacking her face against the ground. An electric shock of pain shot through her skull, her face still bruised, but the ointment the man had given them had taken the edge off.

The glare from the floodlights burned Gracie's eyes. Matilda, Hawk, and the boy with the birthmark all blinked and rubbed their faces, each of them dealing with the violent change from complete darkness.

The plaza might have been lit up like the sun, but it stood empty. The night-time covers were over the other cages, and all the prisoners were quiet.

Gracie jumped when she looked to her right. The gentle man and the pink-haired warrior stood by the cage's door. They had four guards with them, two men and two women. "What's—"

"Shh!" The boy with the birthmark pressed his finger to his lips.

Gracie pointed at the boy. "Tell me to *shh* again and see what happens."

The boy lowered his gaze.

The warrior slipped a key into the cage's lock. Her shoulders rose to her neck, and her face twisted with a wince as she slowly turned it. Her mouth moved as if the action could somehow silence the inevitable *clunk!* The hinges creaked when she opened the door.

"What's going on?"

The boy half-raised his finger to his lips, but stopped short under Gracie's burning scrutiny.

"I'm not sure," Matilda said.

Hawk squinted when he peered from the cage, as if it would help him see through the blinding light. "They're going to take us somewhere."

"This is it." Gracie threw her arms up. "They're done with us now. This is when they get rid of us. I knew we couldn't trust them." She folded her arms across her chest, shook her head, and turned her back on the cage door. "Well, I'm not going anywhere. They'll have to drag me out kicking and screaming."

Hawk said, "Uhh!"

Gracie turned back around. The pink-haired warrior carried a knife, the blade at least a foot long. A crude weapon, the steel buckled and rusty, but the point sharp enough and the blade thin enough to do plenty of damage if she used it on them. The cut would be far from clean, but it would be deep. She pressed her finger to her lips and said, "Shh."

Clamping her jaw so tight her gums ached, Gracie did as the woman instructed. She could have taken the boy in a fair fight. But with her face in its current battered and throbbing state, and with the woman being armed and backed up by guards, she had no chance.

The warrior flicked her knife, instructing Gracie and the others to step from the cage.

Hawk and Matilda stepped out, their shoulders slumped, their heads bowed. Scolded children, they were about to acquiesce and take their punishment.

"If …" The warrior's hard scowl silenced Gracie. Maybe she didn't need to say anything. If she didn't move, they'd soon get it. They were going to kill them anyway, so she might as well stay here and let them kill her in the cage. End it on her own terms. No point in being marched to wherever they were going to take them to them have their throats cut.

"Gracie." Matilda re-entered the cage and raised a gentle hand at the warrior as she passed her. She moved closer to Gracie and spoke in a whisper. "We're going, so please just come with us. You stay here and they'll lock you in this cage again. They might be covered now, but think about how the other prisoners looked. That's your future. Unless you come with us and see where this path leads. I know you don't trust these people, and you have every right not to, but we're screwed anyway, right? We might as well follow them."

Folding her arms tighter, Gracie shook her head.

"My dad saw the worst in every situation," Matilda said.

"You're comparing me to your dad?"

Matilda held Gracie's right hand. "Not in general, no. And not the Gracie I met before Dout fell. You were optimistic then."

"A lot's changed."

"It has. And I'm sorry for what you've been through. But the point I'm trying to make is you're better than my dad. My dad was a cynic. And, like most cynics, he believed himself to be smart. He couldn't see he had the certainty of an idiot. He thought he had it all worked out."

"You're calling me an idiot now?"

"You're struggling to see anything other than a bad ending."

"I know these people."

"You *knew* the people at war with Dout. Not these people. And even then, you thought there might be a better way than fighting. Right now, you sound like your brother."

"Maybe he was right?"

"Maybe he was. But again, if staying in this cage is the end for us, then what have we got to lose by leaving it? You know what I think?"

Gracie shrugged. She'd have to hear it anyway.

"I think my dad was scared and couldn't admit it. Because of that, he needed to feel in control. He needed to make sure he knew how *every* situation would end because he was so petrified of uncertainty. He didn't understand the world better than anyone else. But invariably, he was right."

"So what's your point?"

"Things often ended badly. But those bad endings were all his doing. His self-fulfilling prophecy. Cynics have their eyes shut, not open. They project their fears and insecurities on the world, and when they see a chance to prove themselves right, they double down. They stay in their cage."

Gracie squirmed when Matilda paused.

"Hawk and I are leaving. We both want you to come with us. Before we got caught by these people, you were brave and kind. You had your eyes open."

"I know these people." Even as she said it, Gracie's words lost their strength.

Matilda pulled a tight-lipped smile at her friend.

Gracie closed her eyes and filled her lungs. She rested her palm against her chest. Against her mum and dad's wedding rings. Opening her eyes again, she nodded.

"You'll come?"

She nodded again, fixing on Matilda so she didn't have to look at the murderous bastards outside their cage. "Yes. We're dead anyway, right?"

Matilda threw her arms around Gracie. "Come on, let's go." She led her from the cage.

The bald man, the boy with the birthmark, and the pink-haired warrior walked ahead of them. They led them down the first road on their right. The four guards walked behind.

The place was a maze. A labyrinth. They followed their captors' lead and took left turns and right turns. The massive, cold steel walls flanked them on either side and blocked the moon's light. Why hadn't they just killed them in the cage? Why the need for ceremony?

A wider road gave them a rare glimpse farther ahead. Gracie halted. The guards behind stopped, as did the three in front.

"What is it?" Hawk said.

Gracie pointed into the distance. The moon shone along the tops of the walls and on the vast roof. "That's the place we passed earlier. The stadium. The arena."

Matilda leaned to the side to peer around the three in front. "Oh, shit!"

"I told you this was bad news. I told you we couldn't trust them. That's where we're heading. I can guarantee it. However hopeful you choose to be, Matilda, we're going to be tomorrow's entertainment. And I wouldn't mind betting the odds will not be in our favour."

One guard shoved Gracie in the back, encouraging her forwards. They crossed the wider road and ducked into another series of tight alleys, the arena gone from their line of sight. For now.

"You never know," Matilda said. "They might take us somewhere different."

"When will you wake up?" Gracie said.

"You think I'm not worried about ending up in that place? We can only deal with it when we get there. *If* we get there. I'm going to choose to remain hopeful. If these are my last moments, I'd rather fill them with optimism. We're going to die anyway, right?"

~

THEY TOOK SO many turns and diversions, Gracie's head spun.

"And there it is again," Hawk said.

Only the briefest glance, but they were closer to the arena. "I told you," Gracie said. "Make sure your optimism doesn't cloud your ability to see an opportunity."

"What do you want, Gracie? For me to say *well done*?" Matilda shook her head. "You're right. We're screwed. You win."

They ducked down another alley, the arena gone from their sight again.

They came out where Gracie and the others had been when they first found the arena. The vast corrugated steel roof stretched away from them, the arena sunk into the ground. The five-foot gap between the top of the roof and their feet had windows running along it. It showed them the huge amphitheatre bathed in a dull light. It stood empty for now. Ghostly silence swelled through the place. The invisible audience in the surrounding seats held its collective breath in anticipation of the duels to come. The spectacle that Gracie and her two friends would no doubt be a part of. The humiliation of foreigners who dared to enter their territory.

The path alongside the arena sloped down. Gracie's heart pounded in time with her heavy steps. Matilda held her hand.

The gap from the ground to the arena's roof now tens of feet tall. The place fronted by two massive steel doors that were featureless save for the random chaotic scratches of brushed steel. These gates had nothing on the ones in the wall, but they still stood about thirty feet tall and the same wide. A slit down the middle, they were designed to part and open.

The pink-haired warrior strode up to the doors as if announcing her arrival. But to whom? There were no cameras. No windows for the people inside to peer from. How were they being watched? Who would let her in?

The warrior dropped to her knees, pressed her hands together, palm to palm like she'd done to Matilda after they'd fought, and leaned forward, pressing her forehead to the concrete.

"What's she doing?" Hawk said.

"Who knows?"

The bald man who'd fed them dropped his head to show Gracie and the others the back of his neck. He had a horizontal scar about an inch wide, which he traced with his index finger. He said something to the four guards. They too showed the backs of their necks, and they all had similar scars. While the warrior remained on her knees, the man pointed at her and traced his own scar again.

"She has one too?" Hawk said.

The man nodded like he understood. He grabbed the boy with the birthmark and spun him around so they saw the back of his neck.

Matilda said, "No scar."

"But what does that mean?" Hawk said.

The man pointed at the boy and then at them before pointing away from there.

Gracie tilted her head to one side. "I think it means he's going to take us somewhere."

The man produced more brown bars and handed them over to Gracie and the others before gently shoving them away, after the boy without the scar.

Gracie and her friends followed him, but Gracie kept

glancing behind. When would the guards give chase? When did the sport of hunting them down begin? The pink-haired warrior stood up. Would she lead the charge? But she stayed where she was and waved them away.

"Do you really think they're letting us go?" Matilda said.

"Yeah." Gracie nodded. "Actually, I do."

They came to one of the many white lines in the place. The first one since they'd left their cage. The two lights on the walls on either side flashed red. The boy pointed at the line and then pointed at the back of his neck. He jumped across the line and back again. He gestured back the way they'd come from and shook his head before jumping across the line again and beckoning them on.

Hawk stepped over the line. "I wonder why the others can't cross these lines."

Gracie stepped across next. "If only we'd known that when we surrendered to them. We could have fought our way across the line and been at the guards' block by now."

Matilda's mouth hung open when she looked from one light to the other. "And why are they flashing red?"

Gracie shrugged. "There are a lot of things we don't know about this place, and I'm not sure I care to know. Let go of the need for certainty, right?"

Matilda smiled.

They took several more twists and turns, every alley darker than the one before.

The boy finally stopped and pressed his finger to his lips. He pulled close to one wall and leaned against it. The dark shadows buried him from sight. Gracie and the others copied him.

Clack-clack! Clack-clack! Gracie raised her eyebrows at Matilda. How had he heard that from so far away?

Clack-clack! Clack-clack! The dog galloped past the end of the alley. An awkward see-saw gait, it flashed across and then vanished, fading into the distance. *Clack-clack! Clack-clack!*

The boy waited for silence before he led them away again. Where the dog had gone left, he led them right.

Several turns later, the boy stepped into a shaft of moonlight and pressed his hands together, palm to palm. He bowed at Gracie and her friends. He then walked back the way he'd come from.

"That's it?" Matilda said. "We're free?"

"It looks that way," Gracie said.

The boy didn't look back.

"So what do we do?" Hawk said.

"It's too dark to walk around this place." Gracie pointed at the ground. "This looks like as good a spot as any. I think we should rest until first light and do like we planned."

"Head to the guards' block?" Matilda said.

Gracie shrugged. "Unless you have a better suggestion?"

Matilda smiled again. Some of the colour had returned to her cheeks. "No." Her smile broadened. She sat on the ground, leaned the back of her head against the tall wall, and closed her eyes. "I think that's a great idea."

CHAPTER 25

Joni pulled another ball of meat from her mouth. She used her tongue to force the rest back into her cheek. "Mama Bird started chewing this nice and early so it's moist for you. Easier on your fragile stomach."

Dried and crusty meat fell from his lips when she shoved more in. "This is the better stuff. Mama Bird chewed it into a paste. She knows you might not find it so easy to eat. She's sorry. She will try harder. She'll do better."

Another ball of moist meat, Joni forced it into his mouth after the first lot. "This will—"

His eyes flashed open.

"Wha—!" Joni stumbled, tripped, and fell on her back.

A spew of unintelligible noises. He shook where he lay. He twisted and turned against his bonds. He spat several times, rejecting the food Joni had shoved into his mouth. All the food she'd spent her time chewing.

"Yeargh!" He shook. The wheels on one side of his trailer lifted and crashed down again.

Scrambling backwards away from him, Joni's feet slipped on the damp stone floor. Adrenaline flooded her system, turning her clumsy, and she fell onto her back just as one of his restraining straps broke, freeing his upper body.

He sat up. "What are you?"

"Mama Bird." Joni pushed herself from his room.

"What?" The strap across his waist broke.

"Mama Bird. Here to help you. To make you better."

He slid from the trolley.

Joni jumped up and slammed the door shut. Her hand shook on the key as she fought to twist it.

His steps closed in.

Thunk! She locked the door.

Bang! He slammed into the other side and beat against it. *Thud! Thud!* "Let me out!"

Her arms folded across her chest, Joni shook her head. "That's not what you say."

"Let me out!"

Stars swam in her vision from the force of her reply. "That's not what you say!"

"What? What do I say?"

"I'm hungry. Baby chick's hungry!"

"What are you talking about?" He threw several more thudding attacks against the other side of the locked door.

Joni grabbed the hatch's small handle in a pinch. She held her breath.

Bang!

She jumped back.

Silence.

Joni stepped towards the door again, trembling when she gripped the hatch's handle for a second time. She slid it open. *Thunk!*

His brown eyes appeared at the letterbox slot. Wild, they spread even wider. "Who are you? What are you doing to me? Why was I tied up? Where's Nick?" He spat at her through the hatch. "And what's all this shit in my mouth? What's going on?"

"Mama Bird was looking after you. Taking care of you." She shook when she shouted. "And this is how you treat her?!" Her words echoed in the damp space. They ran down the tunnel to the oubliette.

"Let me out."

"You'll hurt Joni if she lets you out. She wasn't born yesterday. Yes, today, vest today."

"Joni? That's your name?"

"Yes. Today."

His voice softened. Baby chick needed his mama. "Come here, Joni."

Joni stepped forwards.

"Closer. I want to thank you for what you've done for me."

A foot away from the door. Thick steel between them.

His arm shot through the hatch. His fingers scraped her shirt, but he gripped air in a white-knuckled fist. "What have you done to me?" He grabbed in her direction, his hand opening and closing, his rage tearing his words. "Where's Nick?"

Joni pointed at him with a shaking finger. "You tricked Joni. You pretended to be nice to draw her close. Joni can't trust you. Mama Bird might have to turn her back on her baby."

"What are you talking about?"

"Feed you, look after you, and this is how you react. No!" Joni shook her head. "Joni won't let that slide. Ride. Hide. Joni won't let you treat her like this in her own home. No!" She stamped her foot. "No!"

Joni returned to her seat in front of her screens. Her eyes itched with the start of tears. The screens blurred. "Mama Bird just wants to take care of the little ones, and this is what she gets? This is how he repays her? Joni will not go to him. Joni won't put herself in danger again by getting too close."

He watched her from the hatch like a dog. Like a drone. Come close and she'd burn or get filled with lead. "Come here, you lunatic!" *Bang!* He kicked the door. "I'm going to break your neck!"

"Joni's not safe coming here. Here, near, fear. Joni will close her ears." Clapping her hands to the sides of her head, Joni rocked in her seat. "Joni will not come near!"

CHAPTER 26

The lights on either side of the white line continued flashing red. William crossed the thick painted band behind Olga, the hum of his tyres against the rough concrete quietening because of the smoother surface. The brief respite made the constant vibrating drone on the other side all the more jarring. But a small price to pay when weighed next to the benefits of these boards. He leaned forwards, speeding up and pulling next to his friend. Just glad to be moving again. They'd spent a chilly night in the smallest street they could find. They'd camped out close to a white line. The ability to cross one seemed to solve a lot of problems, so they kept that option open. The sun on their left, they were heading for the guards' block again. They'd not spoken much, even after he'd apologised about using Max against her. And why should she talk to him? It was a low blow. "I could get used to having one of these things, you know? It's so much better than walking or running."

Her hands at her sides, Olga veered from the road they were on. She turned left, right, and then left again. The sun back where it belonged, they continued heading south.

The next alley tighter, but it still gave William the space to travel at Olga's side. The collective hum of their wheeled boards resonated in the tight space. "But, if we could move at a slightly slower pace, that would be great. I worry I've got a mistake in me at this speed."

Olga eased back a little.

William copied her. "Thank you. It's hard to follow someone at speed when you don't know where they're going until the last minute."

Squinting against the rising sun and the assaulting head-wind, Olga kept her focus in front of them.

"I'm sorry again, you know. About what I said about Max."

Their slower speed made the next few turns much easier to manage.

"I'm scared," William said.

Olga slowed a little more.

"I'm scared for Matilda and the others."

"But Matilda most of all?"

"She's been in my life for almost as far back as I can remember."

"That's why we need to get to the block," Olga said. "They'll be there. Or they will at least find their way there." Every turn to keep the sun on their left, she took a sharp right, the road like all the others, save for the width. This one, about ten feet across, sat much wider than most. She slowed a little more. "I pushed Max. I thought applying a bit of pressure would help him conquer his fears."

"You always acted with the best of intentions."

Olga scoffed. "Didn't get the best results though."

"You can't control that. Besides, what else were you to do? We didn't help. We were a ticking clock of constant pressure. We wanted you to leave with us."

Around the next bend, Olga halted, but William carried

on. He didn't have her mastery of the board. He finally came to a stop across the entrance to the industrial plaza. The same one they'd killed the guards in. The catapult still in the centre. The guards' bodies still on the ground. A tank, like the one they'd seen when they came over the wall, had parked up beside the catapult. "How did we end up back he—"

A guard's bullet pinged off the steel wall next to him.

William's hands shook as he fumbled for his gun. He returned fire with a spray of bullets.

About eight guards, they all ducked behind the tank.

Olga appeared beside him and backed him up. Her shots kept the guards hidden. "I didn't expect us to end up here again," she said. "I just took us south."

"Maybe it's not the best option."

"Or maybe you should have listened to me in the first place so we wouldn't have had to retrace our steps!"

Another burst of fire, William made their tank sing before he spun around and followed Olga out of there.

Olga took another sharp turn right down a tighter road. Long and straight. Too tight for the guards' vehicle.

Another tank screeched to a halt at the other end, blocking them off.

William, about six feet behind, followed Olga's path when she turned left.

The road wider than the last. The wind cold against William's face. A humming drowned out their wheeled boards. Another tank. He raised his gun but dropped it instantly, following Olga down the next road on the right.

Olga turned again, the road wider still.

Humming tanks in the distance.

Olga slowed. A white line ahead of them. The lights flashed red. "We need to make sure we don't cross any of those white lines."

"What?"

"They know we've killed the guards, Right?"

William shrugged.

"But they've only seen us in this section. They don't know we left and came back. While they're watching us, we need them to think we can't cross the lines. Then—"

"When they're not watching, we can cross one and sneak away."

"Exactly." Olga's hair whipped across her face from where she turned in William's direction. "And we can lose these tanks on the narrower roads."

"You're sure?"

"We did things your way and ended up chasing our tails. You need to let me make the decisions now. Trust me like you'd trust Matilda."

William eased off and opened up a few feet between him and Olga again.

Back at full speed, William remained on Olga's tail. Left, right, straight at a crossroads, left, left, left, right. They shot into a residential area, leaving the tight streets behind them for the even tighter alleys created by the close press of the small houses. They'd lost the tanks. Get through here and they'd find a white line on the other side to cross.

Washing lines hung between some of the squat buildings. William ducked and weaved. He followed Olga's sharp turns. *Thwap!* He collided with a cold and damp sheet and dragged it from the line. Still at full speed, he fought its cloying grasp. He discarded it moments before he nearly hit the next one.

More sheets up ahead. They'd obviously come on the wrong day. Heavy with damp, they tugged on the lines.

Olga avoided the next loaded line. She took them through the tight walkways where the houses backed against one another. They'd slowed their pace to manage the mazy path.

They could afford to ease off. The tanks had no chance of getting through here.

The next street had more drying sheets. Olga avoided it with another sharp turn.

Shouts and screams rang through the residential section. William understood none of it.

On the next wider street, several people ran from their houses and launched damp sheets over their lines. They were doing it on purpose. So much for having a shared enemy.

Olga turned off the road again.

William followed, leaning into his board. "Olg …" The onrushing wind feasted on his words.

"Olg …"

She shot around the next bend, away from him.

William called after her, "Olg—" He rounded the bend and turned his head at the last minute. The rope, made from plaited washing lines, caught him beneath his left ear. It hurled him to the ground. The hard impact forced the air from his lungs. His board shot away. Gasping, he opened and closed his mouth. He clung to his neck, his words trapped in his restricted throat.

A mob up ahead descended on his and Olga's wheeled boards. Men, women, and children, they all wanted them.

Fighting for breath, William sat up. He raised his gun and shot the walls on either side of the people. They froze, then scattered.

William stood. "You okay?"

Olga held up her hands. A red line across her palms. "Sore, but better than being headless, eh?"

William rubbed beneath his ear and helped Olga to her feet. "Come on, I think we've done enough to frighten them off. Let's get out of here."

Back on their wheeled boards with their guns raised, Olga led the way. They rolled onto the wider road running through the community. The people had gone. Every door and window shutter had been closed.

"Come on." Olga sped up and entered another road, the sprawling mess of houses and washing lines behind them.

"Those people must have known we weren't guards," William said.

"Of course they knew we weren't guards."

"What I mean is, they must have had a warning. How else would they have had time to set up that trap for us? They wouldn't have been able to spring us that quickly."

"You think those flashing red lights might have done it?"

It seemed so obvious now. The high-pitched note stole his reply. He raised his left index finger, encouraging Olga to listen. The ring of steel against concrete. The circular bikes were closing in on them. "Great! It seems like every person in this place is out for our blood."

CHAPTER 27

Gracie flinched away from the two people looming over her. She covered her head with her arms. Her face still throbbed. The ointment had made it better, but she couldn't fight again. Not yet.

"Gracie?"

"Matilda?" She pulled her arms down. "Where are we?"

"Who knows?"

The previous evening flooded back, the cold light of day snapping Gracie lucid. "What time is it?"

Hawk paced up and down. He checked one way and then the other. "About an hour after first light."

"Why didn't you wake me?"

"You needed the sleep." Matilda leaned closer. "How are you feeling?"

Gracie touched her face. The surface-layer sting had subsided. Still swollen with bruising, but the raw sensitivity had dulled. She turned to Hawk. "That ointment's good, isn't it?"

Hawk shrugged.

"You still in pain?"

Hawk shrugged again. He'd removed the bandage from his neck. The cut had now scabbed over.

"Have you two been awake since first light?"

Hawk looked up and down the road again. "Yep."

"Okay." Gracie pushed off the cold steel wall behind her and got to her feet. "So we're heading to the guards' block?"

Matilda snapped off a chunk of the sweet brown bar and handed it to her. "Yeah, and hopefully the others are already there."

Gracie put the chunk in her mouth. "I'm going to miss this when it runs out."

"I thought you were going to say you'll miss them," Matilda said.

"You know my thoughts on them. A couple of them were nice, but that doesn't mean they all are."

"But it does mean some are."

A siren wailed. Gracie spun toward the grating cry. The surrounding walls were too high to see over. "Is that coming from the front gates?"

Matilda shook her head. "I don't think so."

"Then where's it coming from?" Several sentry guns sat atop the surrounding walls. Silent guardians ready to dispatch justice whenever they saw fit.

"Who knows?" Hawk turned his back on the sound. "But whatever it is, I think we should go in the opposite direction."

"Unless …" Gracie said.

Hawk rolled his eyes. "Why don't I like the sound of that?"

Gracie turned her palms to the sky. "Unless it's coming from the arena."

"So what if it is?" Hawk pointed in the direction he faced, away from the arena. "We still need to put as much distance between us and it as possible."

"But it's on our way."

"It doesn't have to be on our way. This place is a maze. We could take one of many routes to get to the guards' block."

"Aren't you curious about what was going on with the woman we fought? The way she behaved last night in front of the arena's doors. What was all that about?"

"What if it's crawling with guards?"

"Then we'll leave. How about we vote on it? All those who want to check out the arena, raise your hand."

Gracie raised her hand. Matilda copied her.

Hawk rolled his eyes again.

"You've questioned if this place is right for you, anyway," Gracie said.

"What does that mean?"

"It'll be easier to find your way back to the front gates from the arena. Just retrace the route we took when we first arrived."

"Time in that cage has made me realise something." Hawk's hand went to his neck. He traced his scab with his fingertips. "The ointment helped me make sense of it all. Me talking about leaving this place is about me feeling out of control."

"I think it's made all of us feel that way," Gracie said. "That's because we have been."

"No." Hawk frowned and shook his head. His chest rose with his deep inhalation. The pause lasted a few more seconds before he finally said, "Out of control like I used to feel as a child. When they cut me and gave me an ointment to heal myself, it reminded me of being one of Grandfath—" He lost his words. He scowled at the ground, and his cheeks puffed when he exhaled.

Gracie rubbed his back. "I'm glad."

"You're what?"

"I'm glad you're being honest with us. And I'm glad you

don't want to leave." Matilda nodded along with Gracie's words. "I don't know what it was like for you as a child, but we want you with us, and we're here for you. I, for one, would have missed you had you gone."

Hawk rubbed his eyes. "Thank you. But I'm still not sure the arena is the best place to go."

"I'd say it doesn't matter now." Matilda cupped her ear to show the others they needed to listen.

Footsteps headed their way. An army of people closing in on them.

Matilda pointed back towards the arena. "If we want to avoid them, we have to go that way."

"Where are they going?"

"Maybe the arena too?"

"For what?"

"Exactly," Gracie said. "That's what I want to know."

Matilda moved off, Gracie a step behind. While Hawk was several steps farther back, he still followed. Around a few bends, they came to the white line the boy with the birthmark had shown them he could cross. The lights still flashed red.

They crossed the line and turned down a tighter road about two hundred feet away. They waited, peering back at the line.

About five minutes behind them, and led by guards, the noisy crowd appeared. When they approached the white line, the flashing red lights turned solid white. The guards stood aside, and the people continued on like it didn't exist.

Gracie's jaw fell. "If it's that easy to cross, why were the others so reluctant?"

"I'm guessing the lights changing colour is significant," Hawk said.

"Maybe we should discuss it later." Matilda tugged on

Gracie's arm. "They're going to be on top of us if we don't get away from here."

~

DESPITE TRYING to retrace their steps from the previous evening, they came to the arena from a different angle. A similar spot to when they first found the place, they reached a point where the arena's roof stretched away from them. Gracie checked around before she sat, cross-legged, on the ground directly in front of the windows overlooking the crowd and court. A small gap about six-inches deep ran across the tops of the windows. It released the sounds of the place. The chatter of at least five hundred people. Gracie positioned herself behind a pole just in case any of the crowd turned around.

More people entered the arena. The gates they'd passed the previous evening, the ones the warrior had prayed to, were now open. The people were being instructed on where to go by guards with guns, dogs, and drones. Many of them marched in step and kept their heads bowed.

Matilda leaned closer to her window. "Looks like they were coming here, then."

"Whether or not they wanted to," Hawk said.

The huge steel gates closed behind the small army, and several guards bolted them shut. "Maybe it's fortunate we failed to retrace our steps," Gracie said. "We wouldn't have stood a chance getting past those gates with all that's going on down there."

The new crowd took their seats opposite those already waiting. They matched their opponents in both hostility and number. Hard glares, words fired from one side to the other. Gracie couldn't understand what they said, but she didn't need to. She read their intention loud and clear.

"There must be a thousand people in there," Hawk said.

The crowd's chatter grew louder. The abuse more vehement. Jabbing fingers. Puce faces. Veins standing out on necks.

Two drones flew into the ring and hovered over the plus sign in the centre.

Gracie gasped. "What the …?"

The drones each beamed a prism of needle-thin flickering bars of light into the sky. They made up a moving image of a man's face. In his mid-forties, he had pasty, flabby skin and piggy little eyes. Bald on top, he had ginger hair around the sides of his head that linked from his sideburns to a goatee. His voice was so loud the windows in front of Gracie hummed.

"Ladies and gentlemen—"

"He speaks English?" Hawk said.

"Welcome to this week's fight. Make sure you get your bets in before we start, because the bookies will be closed after that. I'm sure you all know the rules, but for anyone not paying attention, I'll say them again."

Gracie shook her head. "Who's he talking to? They don't understand him."

The man's eyes were dead. His face blank. "Only one champion can be the winner and give their district a chance at the gates. The other might well die."

Many of the crowd sat slack-jawed. Matilda nudged Gracie. "You're right. Look at them. They've got no idea what's going o …"

Gracie followed Matilda's line of sight. Her stomach clenched, and she clapped a hand to her mouth.

"Fighting in the red corner …" the floating head said. "Although, for today, maybe we'll call it the pink corner."

The warrior with pink hair. The one they'd dragged

Matilda from the cage to fight. Gracie spoke through her fingers. "So this is what she was training for."

"And why she let us go," Hawk said. "They were done with us. Now she's going to win or die. Either way, she won't need to continue training."

"It all makes sense now." Matilda shuffled where she sat. "I hope she wins."

Gracie said, "After what they did to us?"

"They set us free."

"They wouldn't have had to set us free had they not imprisoned us in the first place."

"Had the *others* not imprisoned us. This woman and her crew were nice, remember? Who knows what would have happened had they not let us go."

Gracie shrugged. Maybe Matilda had a point.

Hawk pointed to the other side of the arena. "Look who she's fighting."

"And in the blue corner, the favourite." The floating head winked, and one side of his mouth lifted in a smirk. "I think we can all see why."

Well over six feet tall, bald, and covered in deep purple scars. The pink-haired warrior might have had biceps like rocks, but she looked like a child compared to her hulking opponent.

The crowd cheered, the windows shook, and the commentator laughed. He rolled his words, the windows humming again. "Let'ssssss get rrrrrrrreeeeeeady to rumm-mmmmmmble."

"Shit." Gracie lowered her head and sighed.

Matilda raised an eyebrow at her. "Sounds to me like you might want her to win too."

"Maybe they're not all bad." Gracie shrugged. "But Hawk's right. What does it matter? Against that man, she doesn't stand a chance."

CHAPTER 28

Every other road William and Olga approached sang with the hum of chains against concrete. They were surrounded by echoes. Chased by spirits. Whispers of the heavily armed guards on much faster vehicles than them. Make a bad choice and the apparitions they were evading would manifest into something entirely more threatening.

About twenty minutes had passed since they'd first heard them, and they were running out of options. Not a white line in sight because their turns and diversions had twisted them into ever-decreasing circles. How long before they zipped around just a few alleys and tunnels like bugs trapped beneath an upturned glass?

William's abs ached, his core engaged from where he leaned forward to keep pace with Olga.

Olga zipped into another plaza.

William followed and swerved right so he didn't slam into her back or the washing lines. A ten-foot-tall spider's web of plaited nylon waited to bring an abrupt halt to their progress.

And not just one. The residents had hooked up webs

between every building in the place. If there was a route through on their wheeled boards, they had no chance of finding it in a hurry.

Back on Olga's tail, William shot out of the residential area. Back on the narrow streets. The ring of the chains against concrete had faded. They were farther away than they'd been before. "At least we've got some dist—"

A low hum cut William short. "Shit!"

Three guards shot around the bend. All three of them had boards like William's and Olga's.

William fired at them. They were too far away to hit, but it sent them back to where they'd come from.

Olga spun around and zipped off. "We'll find another way."

William leaned forwards and stumbled from his board. He jumped back on and tried again. Nothing. The small light by the right wheel had died. He cupped his mouth with his hands. "Olga!"

She stopped and spun around. Her eyes widened. "Get down!"

William dropped, and she fired over his head. The ting of bullets against steel sent the riders on the boards back around the bend for a second time.

Olga reached William and scowled at his board. "What's up?"

"It's out of power. Look, the light's gone off."

Olga's own light blinked red.

"And I don't think it will be long before the same happens to yours."

"Shit!" Olga jumped from her board. She sent a couple of bullets into the wall close to the guards.

"So what do we do?" William said.

"What else can we do?"

"Huh?"

"We need to go through that residential area. The guards will have to follow us on foot."

"But what about the residents?"

Olga lifted her gun. "That's what these are for. You ready?"

"Yep." Like he'd done for most of this escape, William followed Olga's lead. They ran into the residential section while the hum of the wheeled boards closed in.

Through the first washing-line web, William and Olga turned back towards the entrance, their guns raised.

William's throat dried. The hum from the wheeled boards grew louder. He watched the entrance down the barrel of his gun and pulled the trigger. The humming stopped. A shot of adrenaline wrung his guts. "Uh, Olga."

"Why do I not like that tone?"

"You know those numbers on our guns?"

Olga turned her weapon to look at the red number.

"It's not the number of the soldiers they were assigned to." William's number flashed twelve and Olga's eight. "It's how many bullets we have left."

"Shit!"

"What shall we do?"

"What can we do? We have to make sure they think we still have plenty of bullets."

"And if we can't do that?"

"We die. So we might as well try."

Olga led them through the square. Through the washing-line webs. They took the most direct route to the road at the opposite side of the plaza. Some lines had been tied so tight, William grunted when he tugged them aside.

"Stay there!" Olga pointed her gun at a woman and three children. The children cried, and the woman pulled them all back into a house.

Faces watched them from shadowy alleys. They peered

around the sides of buildings. Just the sight of the guns kept them away.

They exited the plaza and turned left. The hum of the wheeled boards came from their right. "Look!" William pointed ahead. A white line about two hundred feet away. "If we can get across that with no one seeing us, we might get away from here. Come on."

They ran for the line and passed an entrance on their right unlike any other they'd seen. It sloped down into a dark underground tunnel. It looked like a dungeon.

The wheeled boards' hum grew louder. They appeared up ahead. One, two, three of them. This time they shot first, the walls ringing around William and Olga.

William shot back and hit one, knocking them from their board. He had seven bullets left.

The other two dragged their fallen comrade. An arm each, his legs scraped the ground, his boots the last thing to vanish from sight.

Ringing steel called to them. A ghostly whine, as if the walls sang. Bikes! But they were too far away to be of any concern.

Clack-clack! Clack-clack!

Olga's eyes widened.

William sighed. "I didn't think it could get any worse."

Olga nodded towards the white line. "We might cross that line unseen, but I don't think we'll remain hidden for long. Those dogs will be on us."

"And they might have drones with them."

"There's only one option." Olga shot back at the guards on the wheeled boards.

William shook his head. "There must be another way."

"If you have anything else, I'm all ears, but we're running out of time." She tilted her gun to show a red number five. "And ammo."

"Fuck it!" This time William led. He ran down the slope into the darkness of the underground tunnel. No torch and very little ammo. But some small shred of hope in the darkness had to be better than no hope if they remained where they were.

Inside, William leaned against a cold steel wall and strained his ears to listen for the bikes. For the wheeled boards. For the drones and dogs.

What little light made it down there shone off Olga's sweating face. She leaned close to William and whispered in his ear, "They're not following us. Let's get deeper in before they change their minds." She broke into a sprint. She slammed into a transparent wall with a *tonk* and stumbled back while rubbing her head.

William yelped at the face that appeared on the transparent barrier. A floating head. A bald man with red hair around the sides and back. He had a ginger goatee and pasty white skin. "Welcome to the rat run. This is a place of many false exits and only one true escape."

Covering his mouth, William leaned close to Olga and whispered, "He speaks English."

Olga raised her eyebrows.

The floating head laughed. "Unless you call the sweet mercy of death an escape, which is precisely what you deserve. With what you've done to several of my guards, think yourself lucky that we're giving you this opportunity, even if you end up begging to be killed by the time we're done with you."

William pointed back at the daylight shining in from where they'd entered. Again, he covered his mouth. "We should go back."

"Why are we still whispering?" Olga said.

"What if he doesn't know we speak English? I think the longer we can keep that hidden from him, the better.

Remember how those guards we stole the boards from reacted when they heard us?"

Olga whispered back, "If we go out there again, we know we'll die."

The floating head tilted to one side, guided by an invisible neck. "Good luck, little rats. May you find your freedom. Make sure you avoid the tomcat." The face vanished, and the slight shine on the transparent barrier disappeared when it split down the middle and retracted into the walls on either side.

William kept his mouth covered. "You're sure about this?"

"Like with every other choice we've made in this place, it's not a good option, but it seems like the best available. Unless you have a better one?"

William shook his head and stepped through the barrier. Olga followed him.

Thunk! The barrier closed behind them.

Olga pressed against it. It didn't budge. She leaned close to William and covered her mouth. "We couldn't leave now even if we wanted to."

A deep roar shook the walls. The vibration came through the soles of William's boots. He tightened his grip on his gun.

The decapitated head might have gone, but his voice returned. His laughter. He laughed so hard he struggled to breathe. The cackling glee surrounded them in the tight tunnel. In between wheezing gasps, the man said, "Good luck, little rats! Good luck."

CHAPTER 29

Drones circled the arena like massive mechanical hornets. Their guns hung down from their bellies, deadly stingers capable of shutting people down. But the audience paid them no mind. Everyone watched the fighters in the centre. The commentator had told them to fight, but they remained still, fists raised, each waiting for the other to make a move.

The pink-haired warrior charged.

Gracie half-turned away. "That man's going to destroy her."

"You never know," Hawk said.

"Look at the size of him. He's taller, wider, and stronger than her. Even his scars are worse than hers. Like he's fought tougher opponents on his path to get here."

"But he hasn't fought me," Matilda said with a smile. "So she has the upper hand."

The woman landed several clean shots. The echo of each contact whipped around the silenced arena. *Crack! Crack! Crack!*

The man took them with ease.

Matilda sighed and shook her head.

The man moved so fast, the sound of his blow reached Gracie before she registered his punch. *Crack!*

A thunder strike of a hit. The woman's pink fin of a mohawk exaggerated her head's snapping movement. She stumbled, fell, and landed on her arse. Gracie's back twinged in empathy.

Yells lit up one side of the arena. The man's half of the crowd. They jumped and waved. They punched the air. They screamed and shouted.

His massive fists held out to either side, the man strode forwards, stalking her. His jaw worked from where he chewed on the air between them. He threw a kick.

Crack! The woman blocked it with both hands.

He followed with another punch and knocked her flat. He raised his fists to the crowd. The windows in front of Gracie hummed with their vociferous response.

"We need to stop the fight." Gracie rocked forwards to stand and instantly fell back when the man kicked the woman in the stomach. What could they do? They'd be up against drones, guards, and an enormous crowd where half, if not all of them, were hostile.

Gracie slumped against the pillar, still hidden should any of the crowd look back. But they were too busy watching the fight. She shook her head. "She's screwed."

The warrior yelled. His deep roar escaped the small gap above the windows. He turned to his side of the arena and punched the air. They responded with a wave of noise.

The man swung his arms backwards in wide circles, whipping up the crowd. All the while, the pink-haired warrior crawled away, dragging herself along the floor.

The man ran at the woman. A charging rhino. This contact would be the last.

But the crawling woman rolled away, and the man caught air with his heavy boot. Driven by the momentum of his spite, he spun around and ended with his back to her.

The woman jumped to her feet and raised her fists. She stumbled back towards the wall, her own crowd above.

Animated by the woman's proximity, her supporters stamped and roared. They punched the air.

"No." Gracie shook her head. "She doesn't stand a chance."

The man, his face and head a beacon of incandescence, charged again. His teeth bared, he yelled.

The woman widened her stance.

"What are you doing?" Gracie whispered. "Run!"

Hawk's jaw hung loose. "She can't stand toe to toe with him."

But the woman had one advantage over the man. He might have been powerful, but his attacks came from a mile away. She read his punch, dodged it at the last moment, grabbed the back of his shirt, and propelled him into the wall behind her.

Gracie's stomach twisted at the *crack* of the man's head connecting with the wall. Silence fell on the arena.

"That's what I used on her!" Matilda punched the air. "Get in. You go, girl!"

A wild primate, the woman jumped on the man. She'd already knocked him out, but she made sure with a flurry of blows. Her nose bloody, she sprayed crimson spittle while slamming him with punch after punch.

The woman stepped back. Her shoulders rose and fell with her ragged breaths. Her face glistened with sweat. She remained fixed on the man, but the limp body of the fallen beast had nothing left.

"I don't believe it," Gracie said.

Two drones shone their prisms of light filaments into the

sky again. The floating head beamed with a broad grin. "And there we have it, ladies and gents. Our champion. She's just won her district a chance at freedom."

CHAPTER 30

"Let me out, you crazy bitch!"

Joni rapped her knuckles against the side of her head. A woodpecker attack on her skull. She clamped her hands over her ears. She rocked in her chair. "Mama Bird just wants to look after you. Make sure you're okay, and this is how you treat her? How can you be so mean after all she's done for you?"

"You're holding us in here as prisoners."

"No!" Joni jumped to her feet and pointed at the rude boy. "*Not* prisoners. Mama Bird's here to care for you. To make sure you're okay. She has to stay out here and sleep in this uncomfortable seat, the glow of these screens keeping her awake all night." She threw her right arm toward her locked bedroom door. "While your friend takes *her* bed."

The angry boy's voice softened. "What have you done with him? Is he okay?"

"Of course he's okay. Mama Bird's looking after him. All without a word of thanks."

"He's awake?"

"Not a word of thanks!" Joni shook her head. "No matter what Joni does, no one's ever grateful."

The boy's voice echoed in the cavernous space. "What's going on with him? You need to let me see him."

See him like she saw the man in the tower. Watch him. Wait for the right moment. "Joni has to finish him. Silence him for good. She's done with him now." A cold bucket of water in the corner. Sometimes, during the winter, it iced over. She plunged her hand into the frigid liquid and grabbed the knife's handle. The blade more rust than metal, but still thin enough to drive through his ribs. "If a punctured lung doesn't get him, sepsis will."

"Easy!" the boy said. "I'll be quiet, yeah? There's no need to use that."

"Joni will kill him. He'll die with a rusty blade between his ribs. Get what's coming to him for all the horrible things he's done."

"Look, I'm sorry. I didn't mean to be so rude."

"Rusty, dusty, musty." Joni held the blade up to the glow from the screens. "Trusty blade. Watch him fade. Degrade."

"Go on then." His eyes damn near popped from the hatch. "If you're going to do it, do it, you lunatic. End me!"

Joni tilted her head. "Huh?"

"Just do it."

"Do it, knew it, blew it." Joni slipped the knife down the waistband at the back of her trousers. She climbed the rusty ladder rungs embedded in the wall. She pushed the cold and heavy steel hatch aside, the disc scraping over the concrete road above.

She lived in the block's shadow, but far enough away to be left alone. "The only company she gets is when she visits him. Joni won't have to do these little trips anymore when she ends him." The laugh came from deep within her. A rumbling starting in her bowels, she dragged the steel hatch back across, sealing her home. "He's probably moved again. But Joni will find him. She'll stick him with her rusty blade. She's been getting the blade ready for years and years. Waiting for this moment."

Joni stretched to the sky, filling her lungs with the cool air of a new day.

The shadow hid her approach as well as her home. The building sat on top of a garage. A garage with many entrances. And many maintenance shafts. Choose any and she'd be in the steel rat run of tight tunnels. She knew them as well as she knew anywhere in this place. She'd find him. "And when she does, Joni will make him pay."

The garage was open. "The garage is always open. They fear no one. But they should fear Joni. He should. If he knew what was coming to him, he would." Joni ran down the closest ramp.

Dark inside. It stung Joni's eyes to search for guards. "But Joni always searches. Complacency killed the cat. She's no cat. Mama Bird. Mama Bird who'd fight any cat that came for her babies. The natural order doesn't always win."

Past a six-wheeled tank, the steel shell clean and blemish-free. "They don't fight wars. They don't know what a war is. But he will. Joni will bring war to him. War, chaos, assassination."

She passed tanks, hoverboards, bikes. More than they could ever use, but they had the resources, and they needed to make sure they always had the means to keep control.

"Which maintenance tunnel today? Mix it up. Keep him guessing. If there are too many options to guard, they won't guard any. If they even know how Joni gets in. They don't yet know where she lives."

Shouts outside stopped Joni dead. "Huh?" She pressed her back against the rough concrete wall.

Flashing lights threw a pulsing crimson glow through the

place. An alarm sounded. Shrill. Piercing. It pulled Joni's shoulders up to her neck.

Joni chased her breaths. "They've found her. She came back too soon. She should have waited longer."

Clunk! Whir!

The garage doors closed from the top down, thick steel shutters blocking every exit.

Joni jumped on a hover board and leaned into it. She shot towards the closest way out. Towards the ever-reducing gap.

Ten feet of space.

Eight feet.

Six.

She hit the bottom of the exit ramp.

Five feet.

She squatted, ducked the closing door, and shot back out towards her home. But she stopped short. "The alarms aren't for Joni, but people must be watching now. What if someone's watching her? What if they see where she lives? She needs to get out of here. Come back later. She should have brought her scanner. How will she track the drones and dogs? Use her ears. She has ears. She can stay out of their way. She has to. Go back home now and the game's up. They'll all know where she lives."

Thunk! The garage doors closed. Joni shot away down a road on her left.

The wind whipped across Joni's ears. It tugged on her hair, dragging on her ponytail. She tried to grab the handlebars, but this wasn't her wheeled board. "Same principle. Joni knows what she's doing. She can drive these things."

The change in acoustics from where Joni passed entrances to alleys and roads on her left and right. The hum of tyres against the rough ground. The rough ground that would tear the skin from her body if she fell. "But she won't. Joni's doing fine."

Shouts came from the main road. Joni slowed, rolling to the end of an alley. She peered out.

Kids. The lot of them. From about twelve years old to about twenty. Five hundred, if not more. The main road led down to the guards' block. The small army was packed in from one wall to the other. Joni far enough away to be safe. She saw over the tops of their heads. The block in front of them had gone into complete lockdown. Garage doors closed. The solar panel spines that normally stretched away from the building to drag in as much power as possible were now flat against the walls as an armoured outer shell. Joni felt for the knife at her back. "Joni will get him. If they don't first." She sighed. "Who's Joni kidding? They don't stand a chance. Poor, poor bastards."

The kids on the road might have thought they turned up like an army, but they looked like a mob. No synchronicity. They had numbers, the energy of youth, and will on their side. A poor substitute for armour and brains. But what did they have left? They were desperate.

Slingshots, spears, swords, and bats. "Did no one tell them this is a gunfight?"

A boy led the pack of five hundred. Half his face shock white with a birthmark. He shouted at the troops and crashed his sword against his shield. The *crack, crack, crack* of the bent steel against wood stressed his points. Whatever they were. "Joni doesn't understand them, and they don't understand Joni. Enemies because of their dialect. But could she go down there? Get them to listen? To turn around. Go to ground? They're not standing pound for pound. Gram to pound. Moths to flames."

Joni rapped her knuckles against her temple. "What good will it do? They don't understand Joni, and Joni doesn't understand them. Just another person to fight. They'll—"

Clack-clack! Clack-clack!

"Oh no." Joni leaned back on her hoverboard and shot away from the main road, reversing around the corner and out of sight. "Only one winner. Dog's dinner."

The hum of drones accompanied the dogs. They shot past, closing in on the army.

Joni returned to her previous spot. Ten to fifteen dogs and drones descended on the mob. The drones opened fire, spraying bullets at the kids' backs.

They screamed. The back line turned to face them. The rest charged at the building.

Spears, swords, and slingshots rose. The drones' bullets ate through the first line of defence. Boys and girls fell, the dogs cremating those who remained.

At least four hundred of them charged the block.

Another burst of fire. The flash of a gun from one of the many small slots beneath the armoured flaps. The closed solar panels. Another flash of gunfire up to the right. Then more. Stuttered bursts. The drones took them down from behind; the guards took them down from the front.

The screaming silenced in less than a minute. The mob quietened by white-hot bullet fire and red-hot flames.

Spears, slingshots, and swords had fallen with those wielding them. Their weapons no more than a gesture. Ornaments.

Joni sank where she stood.

"Another army down. No." Joni shook her head. "Not an army. These kids are victims. Victims like everyone else here. Victims of his sadism. But Joni has a rusty blade with his name on it."

The sunlight glistened off the blood running towards the block. One strong rain would wash away the memory of these children. They'd been nothing more than target practice.

"And it doesn't end here." Joni sniffed against her running nose. She rubbed her sore eyes. "Someone will pay a heavy price for what's happened today. What kind of self-respecting dictatorship would this be without swift and violent retribution?"

CHAPTER 31

A heartbeat bassline throbbed through the place.

Gu-gung! Gu-gung! Gu-gung!

Every pulse twisted William tighter. He turned on the spot in the gloom. A glint of light above. He grabbed Olga's arm and pointed up.

"So you've seen the cameras." The floating head had turned into an omnipotent voice that resonated through the long, dark tunnels.

Gu-gung!

"Of course we have cameras. How else are we supposed to keep tabs on you? Time's ticking, little rats. You have two hours before we reveal your location to the tomcat. If you've not found the exit by then, you might as well give up. No one has ever gotten away from Old Tom."

A lion's roar called through the place. It buried the throbbing heartbeat.

Olga's cheeks puffed. Her eyes widened. The roar's echo searched the long tunnels. It revealed the labyrinthine sprawl. Showed them a hint of what lay ahead. She leaned closer to William. She still spoke in a whisper. "Any ideas about how we might get out of here?"

William turned his palms to the dark ceiling.

The glass doors they'd just entered through parted again. Light shone into the place. An invitation to return. But what waited for them outside? Another gunfight? They didn't have enough bullets. They could either face a battle they'd lose, or the uncertainty of the darkness ahead. William cupped his mouth. "I guess they're giving us one last chance to change our minds."

Gu-gung!

"It's a trick. This entire place is a trick."

"How do you—"

A ticking clock rode the gaps between the thudding heartbeats. Then a collective swell of metallic chattering. Thousands of steel shards sliding down a hill. A wash of white noise. It came from behind. From farther back than the daylight. From a darkness more complete than what lay ahead.

Immobile, dumbstruck, William stared back.

The abyss morphed into something more. Still dark, but flickers of light slashed through the gloom. Metallic reflections from where they drew closer to the daylight.

With each throbbing beat and each ticking second came more reflected flashes. Tiny sparks. Glimmers of hope. No, William shook his head. This place didn't know the meaning of hope. The hope would kill them.

The lights revealed the glints as a constantly shifting metallic wall. Thousands of tiny parts contributed to the whole.

They passed through the glare from the outside world. It lit them like a shattered window. Thousands upon thousands of tiny insects. They packed the tunnel. As dense as a mudslide.

Olga took off, and William ran after her.

Gu-gung! Gu-gung!

A deep roar ahead. They were running straight at the tomcat. Being driven into it like frenzied sled dogs launched from a cliff.

Olga ran on, but William halted. The wall on his right glistened like a camera lens. A sheet of glass.

Seven bullets in his gun. William sent them back into the bugs. It disturbed the thick swell. It opened a space, which closed as quickly. But it made Olga pause.

William pointed at the glass wall. They couldn't outrun these things.

Olga came back.

Gu-gung! Gu-gung!

William pressed against the cold glass. It held. The chatter of wings now damn near deafening. They drowned in the noise. Why had he called Olga back? He pressed again, his lungs tight. The bugs were about one hundred feet away.

Olga slammed the butt of her gun against the glass. It bounced back with a hollow *tonk!* She spun on the bugs and unloaded. Five bullets. Ineffective. They were both out of ammo.

Gu-gung!

William slapped his palms against the transparent wall and pushed again.

The metallic insects were fifty feet away.

Gu-gung!

Olga kicked it. *Click!* It popped towards them. It had opened by an inch.

William grabbed the door and pulled it wide. He let Olga in first and pressed in after her. But he couldn't close the door. No handle.

In the alcove, blind to the insects' approach, William pulled the door towards him and ripped his hands in at the last. The door remained open by a slit. A slit large enough for a thousand tiny bugs. He grabbed the edge. Something tickled his palm. A piece of string, thin and almost transparent. Like fishing wire.

The clicking wings were almost upon them.

Fighting his own trembling hands, William pinched the wire and lifted it away from the door.

Gu-gung! Gu-gung!

The cloud of metal bugs threw them into total darkness just as William sealed them in with a soft *click!*

Thousands of tiny insects passed them like floodwater. A thunderous wash. A twisting and turning cloud of chaos. The bugs played a ticking symphony against the other side of the glass.

Light flooded back into the place with the passing of the dense cloud. William's heart beat in time with the bassy throb.

Gu-gung! Gu-gung! Gu-gung!

The chatter of small wings snapped William rigid. One in the alcove with them. It fluttered in the small space. "Ow!" He clapped his hand to his stinging cheek where the thing brushed against him.

Olga snapped the butt of her gun into the air. Millimetres from breaking William's nose. She stamped on the bug when it hit the ground. *Thwack!*

William covered his mouth and whispered, "They would have torn us to shreds."

Her lips pursed, Olga raised her eyebrows.

"Well, well!" The omnipotent voice returned. "Check out you two. Looks like we have some smart little rats in the tunnels today. Not only have they killed some of my guards, but they've passed the first test. However, this is only the first. You have one hour and fifty minutes and a looooong way to go. Good luck."

Olga shrugged and pressed the door on the same spot she'd kicked. It swung open into the long and gloomy hallway.

Stepping out after her, William discarded his gun and drew his sword. Little point in having both. Olga did the same. She nodded. Whatever came their way, they'd be ready.

CHAPTER 32

Gracie laughed. "I still can't believe she did it."

Matilda positively beamed. Straightening her back, she lifted her chest. "And with my tactic, might I add."

Hawk scanned their surroundings. "It almost makes our incarceration worthwhile."

"It certainly served their purpose," Gracie said.

Matilda said, "And they did the decent thing and let us go after."

Gracie raised an eyebrow. "I would have rather they hadn't imprisoned us in the first place."

Another check around, Hawk looked over one shoulder and then the other. "Do you think we should get out of here? There are a lot of people in that arena who need to go somewhere. I'd like to be long gone before that happens."

Matilda crouched in front of the windows and peered back inside. "Uh, something's happening down there."

"Something?" Hawk said.

Gracie crouched down too. The doors to the arena hung open. Forty to fifty guards had entered. Flanked by dogs and drones, they walked with their guns raised.

The two distinct crowds on either side of the arena fell silent. Any sound would attract unwelcome attention. From the scowls on the guards' faces, any attention would be unwelcome.

One guard led the line with the stock of his gun resting in his shoulder. He stared down the barrel at the pink-haired champion, flicking his gun to back up his instruction. "Get down!"

She raised her hands in the air.

Gracie shook her head. "She doesn't understand."

Matilda kept her voice low. "It's hardly surprising they hate English speakers if this is how they're treated."

Her thighs sore from crouching, Gracie fell forwards onto her knees. "All right, you've made your point."

The lead guard flicked his gun again. "Get down!"

Her hands still raised, the woman shrugged.

"Get down!" He pointed his gun at her face and then at the ground. He shook with the force of his repeated command. "Get. Down!"

The pink-haired warrior dropped to her front and lay on the ground.

The man grabbed her hands and dragged them to the back of her head. She linked her fingers.

Keeping her in his sights, his voice echoed through the near-silent arena. "Get the others out of here. Now!"

Twenty to thirty soldiers ran to the crowd who'd come to support the losing fighter. They shouted orders that fell on uncomprehending ears, but the gestures that accompanied their cries served their purpose.

"Get up now."

"Get in the ring."

"Move it!"

It took less than a minute to get the five hundred spectators gathered in the centre of the arena. Those seated on the other side looked at one another and spoke in hushed tones. Their palpable anxiety tied Gracie's guts into knots.

About ten guards formed around the five hundred in the centre. One pumped the air with her gun-holding hand. "We're taking you back. Follow me!"

Hawk hunched down near Gracie and Matilda. "We really should get out of here."

"You're right." But before Gracie stood up, the guard who held the pink-haired woman at gunpoint kicked her in the side. The hollow boom of his boot slammed against her ribcage.

Matilda sucked in air through her clenched teeth. "So that's what you get for winning around these parts?"

Two more guards jogged over. The first kicked the woman in the face. Her head snapped to the side, and her body turned limp. The next removed himself from his trousers and urinated on her.

Gracie clapped her hand across her mouth. "Fucking hell!"

The remaining crowd cried and gasped.

"We need to do something," Matilda said.

Hawk threw his arms up in a shrug. "Like what?"

"I dunno. But she won fair and square, and they're doing this to her? That isn't right."

"What can we do?" Hawk said.

The guard who'd kicked the woman and the one who'd urinated on her grabbed her. An ankle each, they dragged her out through the open doors.

"Maybe we can't do anything." Gracie pointed down at the guards and the limp warrior. "But we have to at least try. She doesn't deserve this."

Matilda nodded. "I agree. Let's see if we can help."

CHAPTER 33

"More children dead, and for what? What did they achieve? What will happen now? There will be consequences. There are always consequences. This needs to stop." Joni paced her small room, the screens providing the main light in her damp and dingy home. "But what can Joni do about it? She can barely look after two little chicks, let alone an entire army. And even then, one chick might well die. Too many cuts. What can Joni do for an army? A mob? Maybe she only has it in her to break things. To destroy and torment. To be a nuisance. This is the way around here. They fight. They get killed. A reminder that the house always wins. That he always wins."

The furious eyes at the open hatch watched Joni pace. They followed her one way along the room and back again. "What are you talking about, you lunatic?"

"Lunatic, Mama to a chick, deep thick, twisted brick."

"*What?*" *Bang!* He kicked the other side of the door. "Just let us out. What have we done to you? You're talking about someone deserving something. How do we deserve this madness? What have we done so wrong to end up here?"

Joni spun on the open hatch. She rapped her knuckles against the side of her head. "But the little chick isn't ready. Needs to understand he needs more time. Always more time."

"We don't *have* more time. We need to get out of here. *You* need to let us out."

"There's always time. Joni knows. Joni's been here for years. The one thing Joni has is time." She paused and fixed on the screens. Although he continued his rant, it faded in Joni's mind. Pushed aside by what played out in front of her. On the screen in the top right corner. "Rat run, bat run, fat pun, cat bun."

"Why won't you listen to me?" The little chick kicked the door again.

Joni walked in circles, one eye on the screen. "Rat run. Rat run."

"What are you watching?" He moved to the right side of the hatch.

"Ha!" Joni pointed at him. "He wants to see it. But if he shouts at Mama Bird in this way, he won't see anything. He'll have to be a lot nicer to get a dignified response. Earn respect and that's what you get. Otherwise, he can burn in hell. Rot in a cell."

"Look." The eyes softened, and his voice quietened. "I'll be nice, I promise. I'll stop shouting. I'm scared and angry. If I promise to treat you better, will you show me?"

"Show him? Know him? Trust him? Must win." Joni pointed at him again. Her long finger trembled. She always trembled. "Joni's seen things. Too many things. The box is too small to put it all back in. The contents have spilled everywhere. All over the floor. A big mess that no one will tidy. Much like down here. Supplies from your room all over the place. All the way down to the oubliette. Bric-à-brac.

Stack on stack." She turned the bank of screens towards the eyeballs in the hatch.

The little chick gasped.

"You know them?"

"No."

A quick response. Lightning quick. Something to hide? But what? Who? "Friends of yours? Come here with you, did they? Over the wall? The tall wall. But they didn't fall? Found another way down. To the ground. And now they've found themselves in the rat run."

"What's the rat run?"

"Bad place." Joni shook her head. She folded her arms. "Joni doesn't enjoy going there or even seeing what they do there. No hope in the rat run." She raised a finger. "But they have one advantage no other runner has ever had!"

"What is it?"

"The lines. Don't cross the line."

"What?"

"They'll be fine. Every time." She drummed her fingers against her chin. "This might just work. Then there will be more chicks for Mama to care for."

The eyeballs moved from side to side with his shaking head. "You leave them alone, you nutter."

"Nutter butter. Mama has a purpose. Something other than destruction. Maybe she doesn't need to hurt him. Maybe she's been put here to care for little baby chicks. To help them fly once again." Joni's face tightened. "So many years of hate and anger. She can start to care. To nurture. To look after. She can be the best at that. Invest in that. Rather than hate. Rather than wanting to kill all the time. She's the best mama bird there ever was. She's ready."

"Leave them alone. Please."

"Hush now, little chick." Joni walked to the door, and his arm shot out towards her. She jumped away and ripped the knife from the back of her trousers. She waved it in his direction. Bared teeth, she hissed at him.

His arm retreated. A tentacle from a wounded octopus hiding in a hole. Retreating from an apex predator. He'd best learn his place fast. Only one walked away from this fight. She reached for the hatch and slammed it shut. *Thunk!* "Mama Bird knows what's best. Mama Bird can handle this."

CHAPTER 34

Gu-gung! Gu-gung!

William leaned closer to Olga and covered his mouth. "How long have we been in this tunnel?"

"It feels like days." Olga looked behind her. "But I reckon it's less than half an hour. I'm just not convinced we've made any progress."

A light flashed at the end of the tunnel. A brilliant strobe. It burst to life with a magnesium glare and then died. It left floaters in William's eyes. Again, he covered his mouth and lowered his voice. "What's that?"

Gu-gung!

The man's omnipotent voice beat Olga to it. "You need to get to the light, little rats. Time's running out."

William threw an arm across Olga, halting her before she took her next step. The flash of light might have died, but the memory remained. The floor had glinted like the glass door covering the alcove. He pointed down. Another glass sheet. A trapdoor.

Olga raised her eyebrows and blew out her cheeks with a hard exhale.

William jumped the transparent panel. He landed flat-footed on the other side. He covered his mouth again. "We need to take our time—"

Gu-gung!

"—because the second we rush is the second we'll end up stepping on one of those panels. Do that, and who knows where we'll end up."

As if he'd heard them, the omnipotent voice said, "You now have twenty minutes."

Olga frowned, her jaw tightening from where she clearly fought to hold on to her reply.

"You need to get out of here before that timer runs out."

William shook his head. He walked at the same pace as before. Olga matched his stride. They wouldn't let the voice bully them into running. Into making a mistake.

Gu-gung!

A flash of red shot past them. It raced along both walls and crashed into the end with another explosion of brilliant white light.

Gu-gung! The heartbeat quickened.

Another streaking flash of red.

Another explosion of light.

Gu-gung!

"Just hold your nerve, Olga. We'll get through this. We won't let them bully us."

Gu-gung!

A booming roar behind. It left a tinnitus ring in William's ears and a tremble in his legs.

Gu-gung!

Heavy galloping steps joined the pulsing bassline.

Gu-gung!

Red lightning overtook them again.

A white strike at the end of the tunnel.

Thunderous steps hundreds of feet behind.

Gu-gung!

Adrenaline surged through William. It dared him to run. Beside him, Olga chewed on her bottom lip.

Gu-gung!

She looked back and froze.

A silhouette of the roaring creature. As big as a horse. Its eyes burned with the same crimson glow as the lightning shooting past them.

Gu-gung!

Another earthquake roar.

Red lightning.

A white strike at the end.

Gu-gung!

Olga set off quicker than before. The red lightning reflected off the transparent panels on the ground. She jumped the next one.

William followed.

The heartbeat quickened.

Gu-gung!

His own beat in time with it.

Gu-gung!

The galloping thunder of the tomcat still hundreds of feet behind.

Red lightning.

White strikes.

Gu-gung!

Olga broke into a jog.

William followed.

Gu-gung!

They quickened into a sprint. The red lightning guided their way. They jumped the panels on the ground. They were getting closer to the white strikes.

The omnipotent voice came through again. “Tick! Tick! Tick!” It faded with his cackling laughter.

But they were closing in on the white strike. They'd get there.

The galloping tomcat was still a gargantuan silhouette. They could outrun it. They were fast enough.

Gu-gung!

Glass popped beneath the tomcat's steps when it passed over the panels William and Olga had jumped. Step on one and they'd vanish through the ground. And what then? Where next?

Gu-gung! Gu-gung! Gu-gung!

Jump after jump. Sheet of glass after sheet of glass behind them.

Red lightning.

White flash.

William overtook Olga. The white flash close. So close it dazzled him.

Thunk! William slammed into an invisible wall. He stumbled and fell on his arse. His ears rang. The glass flashed white when the red lightning hit it.

Gu-gung!

Olga shoved the glass barrier open.

Gu-gung!

The tomcat silhouette was now tens of feet behind.

Gu-gung!

Red lightning streaked away.

A white flash in the distance. Another destination. Miles away.

William took Olga's offered hand and got to his feet.

The red lightning revealed the galloping tomcat. Glowing crimson eyes. Black wire fur. Wide jaws with steel teeth. Thick shoulders. It filled the tunnel and closed in on them with a mechanical lolloping gait.

The omnipotent voice laughed. "In less than a minute, you'll be Old Tom's next victim."

Olga dragged William through the door he'd slammed into. They sprinted along the corridor. They jumped the first glass sheet on the ground. The red lightning raced them, overtook them, and crashed into what would no doubt be another glass barrier. White glare. Hundreds of feet away.

The tomcat roared, and William damn near lost his legs.

Gu-gung!

It would catch them before they reached the next door. They needed another plan.

CHAPTER 35

Gracie led them back along the route they'd used to get to the arena. They crossed the white line. The lights atop the walls were out again. Whatever they'd flashed red for had clearly been dealt with.

The end of their path opened onto the main road. Gracie, Hawk, and Matilda hid, peering down at where the guards had parked. A cluster of small vehicles and five tanks, each tank with a huge trailer attached. They were about two hundred feet away. A thick white line ran across the road between them. The guards led the pink-haired warrior's spectators into the trailers. They drove those who weren't fast enough forwards with kicks and punches.

They dragged a woman in her late sixties to early seventies from the line. Three guards set on her, knocking her down before they kicked her limp. One guard ended the attack by stamping on the back of her head with a deep *crunch!*

"Jeez!" Hawk turned away. "Why are they doing that?"

Gracie spoke through a clenched jaw. "Because they're animals."

Tears streaked Matilda's cheeks. She shook her head. "Animals wouldn't do that."

The guards closed the first of the five trailers. It contained about a fifth of the crowd. A tank towed it away.

As many children as adults in the crowd. They filled the second truck and then the third. A mother and child got separated, the mother shouting and reaching out to her little girl. A guard dragged the child from the vehicles, forced her to kneel, and shot her in the back of the head. The mother released a primal, soul-tearing wail while a tank dragged her trailer away.

Gracie's heart ached, and a lump clogged her throat. The small body lay face down against the concrete.

The guard who'd shot the kid sent a burst of bullet fire into the air. "You're all savages. You have nothing but hatred in your hearts. It's a part of who you are. You don't deserve to breathe the same air as us. We try to look after you, and see what happens? Well, this is your punishment. You've earned it, you vile cretins."

Gracie bowed her head. Her tears fell to the rough concrete ground. She flinched when Matilda touched her back.

"You were never that bad," Matilda said. "You were scared. With the life you lived, and what you saw of these people, that's understandable. But you were never malicious. You're a good person."

"Who's said some awful things."

"We all need to be given the opportunity to grow and learn."

The guards filled two more trailers and towed them away. Just one remained. The people from the arena sobbed and wailed. Even through her blurred view, Gracie picked out the bald man who'd fed them from the cage. The one who made the boy take them across a white line to safety. She'd not seen the boy.

The bald man made a break for it.

"You!" a guard shouted and raised their gun. Another guard pushed it down and laughed.

Gracie, Matilda, and Hawk pulled back into the road they'd peered from. The man's footsteps drew closer. Closer to them and closer to the white line. From where they stood, they were away from the guards' line of sight, but they had a view of the thick line on the road.

The man crossed it and coughed a spray of red mist like he'd been shot. But there hadn't been any gunfire. The life left his still sprinting body, his legs bandy, his eyes crimson like a diseased. Still on his feet, blood ran down his face in a waterfall of scarlet tears. His nose bled like a broken tap. His ears haemorrhaged. His legs failed him, and he landed face first. Blood pooled beneath him. Even the back of his light trousers were soaked.

Every atom in Gracie's body urged her forwards. Out into the open to help the man who had helped them. To take on the laughing guards. But what would it achieve?

Matilda clamped her hand across her mouth. It muffled her words. "If he was prepared to do that to get away, what does that say about where they're taking them?"

"We have to help," Gracie said.

The guards had turned their backs on the man and the white line. Focused on the last truck, they pulled about fifteen people from the back. Those inside screamed words Gracie couldn't understand.

When the small group was about fifty feet from the truck, a guard raised his right hand. His thumb rested on a small button. "One of you tried to run, so fifteen of you get punished."

The people in the truck shouted louder.

The guard pressed the button. As one, the small crowd coughed and spluttered. Some sent clouds of red mist into the air. Some doubled over, screaming and holding their stomachs. All fifteen turned limp and fell like the man who'd crossed the line. All fifteen hit the ground and bled from every visible orifice and no doubt the hidden ones too.

The guards laughed. The people in the truck fell silent.

While the rest of them got into the tank, another guard closed the doors to the trailer with a *crash!* He then joined his colleagues.

The hum of the last tank pulled the final trailer away.

Hawk shook his head. "How can we help them?" He stepped from the road. His arm shot up, and he pointed in the direction the tanks had headed. "Wait! I think I know."

Gracie came to Hawk's side. It took all her will to ignore the dead man in the road and the fifteen farther along. The trucks had gone, but a pair of smaller four-wheeled vehicles remained.

Hawk said, "I reckon I can drive one."

"Where are the guards?"

Matilda peered around the corner with them. "Probably still in the arena."

"So if we're going to take them," Hawk said, "we need to do it now."

Gracie nodded. "I'm game."

Copying her gesture, Matilda said, "Me too."

CHAPTER 36

"Run faster, little rats."

The ground shook beneath William's steps. The tomcat breathed down their necks.

Gu-gung! Gu-gung! Gu-gung!

No gaps between the heartbeats. William's own in this throat.

Red lightning.

White flashes.

They jumped transparent panels. Each one the tomcat passed over shattered with a loud *splash!*

Gu-gung! Gu-gung! Gu-gung!

The massive beast snorted and grunted. A mechanical monstrosity covered in red rust. Red rust or dried blood. Its steel jaws would turn them to paste. The size of a horse. The charging force of a rhino. They had no chance. Another roar. It cut through William.

Olga jumped the next panel and pointed down. "This tunnel's never-ending."

William shrugged. What else could they do?

She jumped onto the next sheet of glass. *Pop! Splash!* It turned into a thousand pieces, and she dropped.

William jumped in a second later, the wind from the tomcat's snapping jaws against his back. It missed him by inches. A massive steel paw reached down after him. He crashed into Olga at the bottom of the slide.

The bubbling laughter of the omnipotent voice. "You picked the wrong slide. You had a choice of many. One of them would have given you freedom. This wasn't it."

Daylight ahead. A white line across their path.

"And know the tomcat hasn't given up, little rats. You have two choices. You either cross the line, or you wait for my little pet to find you. This is what happens when you kill my guards. This is what you get. It was nice knowing you, little rats."

"Likewise."

The voice gasped. "You speak English? Who are you?"

Gu-gung!

"Fuck you!" Olga flipped the bird to no one in particular. "Fuck you and your silly little games." She crossed the line.

William followed, his shoulders pulling into his neck. It didn't matter how many times they'd crossed these lines, he always expected something awful to happen.

A helmeted woman appeared about fifty feet away. She had long blonde hair, but her tinted visor hid her face. She pointed above the rat run's exit at the mounted camera. She pressed a finger to the part of her helmet that covered her lips, and beckoned William and Olga over.

Olga led the way again.

"Come with me if you want to live."

"Who are you?"

"No time for that." The woman shook her head for longer than someone should. It was like she couldn't stop once she'd started. "You coming or what?"

What other choice did they have?

"Yeah." Olga nodded. "And thanks."

"We're not safe yet. Now come, let's go before he gets here."

CHAPTER 37

Gracie's grip ached from clinging on, but if she relaxed for even a second, Hawk's erratic driving would fling her from the back of the buggy.

Hawk eased off the accelerator and finished their journey in a similar way to how the rest of it had gone … with a jolt, the front of the vehicle crunching into the steel wall.

Jumping off, her fingers sore, Gracie backed away from the buggy, and Matilda took the words from her mouth.

"What the fuck?"

Scores of severed heads on dirty steel spikes. The one closest to them belonged to a girl, her long black hair matted with her own blood. They'd rammed the spike through the bottom of her neck and punctured the top of her skull. Flecks of white bone stood out among the damp, lumpy matter on her crown. A sea of bodies carpeted the ground. Many had been decapitated. All of them were kids. Many younger than Gracie. Many as young as twelve.

The trucks with the trailers were about two hundred feet away on the other side of the massacre. Parked outside what would normally be a huge building, but it stood in the shadow of the vast guards' block. An entire town within one massive black structure. It had the same feeling as the wall. Like it had been constructed by giants. The same grey steel. Hundreds of windows, each one with its own open shutter that poked away from the building like the spines of a strange fruit. Each shone with a reflective solar panel.

The concrete glistened in the daylight, the ground slick with spilled blood. Gracie filled her lungs. Hopefully the extra oxygen would push her on. She led the way, pressed against the steel wall on her left. She proceeded with cautious steps. Every face on every severed head wore a twisted grimace of horror. Every spike glistened, coated in the leaking fluids of a fresh decapitation. They closed in on the guards and the large steel warehouse into which the guards led the prisoners. The bend in the path hid them from sight. For now.

Gracie jumped when Hawk tapped her on the shoulder. She slowed down and leaned back to better hear him.

"There are steps and walkways around the outside of that warehouse. Let's get to those. Hopefully, it'll help us see what's going on inside."

Gracie looked back at Matilda, who shrugged.

"Oka—" Gracie's already tight stomach clamped. A chill snaked through her. "Shit!" The boy with the birthmark. Or rather, his head. On a spike. His mouth stretched wide in a silent scream. She pointed at him and turned back to the others.

Hawk nodded. Matilda's eyes glazed. What could they do for him now?

Her hands shaking, Gracie gripped the head by pressing her palms to his ears. Her strength nearly abandoned her when she lifted it from the spike. *Squelch.* She laid the head on the ground and winced against her own writhing revulsion. Fixed by the glassy stare of one of their saviours, she backed away until she hit the wall.

"Be at peace," Hawk said to the bodiless boy. "And thank you for what you did for us."

A lump in her throat, Gracie stumbled on.

One hundred feet from the warehouse, Gracie, Hawk, and Matilda waited. Four sets of double doors led into the place. One loud *clack* after the other from where the guards locked each set from the outside. Most of them made their way to the vast building next door. The few who remained entered the trucks and drove them around the back.

"It looks clear," Gracie said.

Hawk and Matilda nodded.

Gracie took off, remaining close to the huge steel wall on their left. Where the straighter stretch of road exposed them, the wall's deep shadow gave them enough cover.

Around the side of the warehouse and out of the block's line of sight. Out of the field of vision of the cameras above the four sets of doors. If they'd made it this far unnoticed, they were home free. But who knew if they'd been seen or not. Without breaking stride, Gracie ran up the metal stairs attached to the building.

Treading light steps while fighting her rampaging adrenaline, Gracie climbed to the top, thirty feet from the ground. A gap where the warehouse's wall met the pitched steel roof. She poked her head through.

There were about five hundred people packed into the space like cattle. Gracie scrunched her nose from the reek of the place. The palpable fear damn near choked her. These people knew their fate.

Matilda appeared next to Gracie. "What are they going to do to them?"

"Whatever it is"—Hawk a little farther along—"it doesn't look good."

Two drones projected an image into the air again. The illuminated head. Bodiless like the others, but it didn't have a spike rammed through it. The same head they'd seen at the fighting arena. Bald on top, ginger hair around the sides and back. He had a ginger goatee, pasty white skin, and the lifeless glare of a sadist. Until it became time to perform.

"Ladies and gentlemen"—he lit up like the plaza's floodlights—"welcome to the warehouse. It's been a busy day. We've had the rat run. A fight. A group of illegals attacked us. And now it's time for this. We don't like to use the warehouse, but if we gave this group of people a chance to run for freedom after the attack on our home, they'll think they've won, and what kind of example will that set?" His pasty face turned puce. "We will not stand for these acts of violent rebellion. So we have another warehouse event for you all. Now, to all those inside the place, what is our mantra?"

Five hundred faces stared at the floating head. Five hundred people and not a single response.

"Tough crowd! Well, viewers, as you all know, *it only takes one.*"

Despite the dense press of bodies in the crowded warehouse, they'd left a circular space in the centre at least fifteen feet in diameter. Marked by a thick white line like those throughout this place. It encircled a red button on a pedestal.

"If anyone presses the button, they're home free. The doors will open, and everyone can leave."

A man yelled. His cry damn near shook the walls. He crossed the line on his way to the red button. His legs failed him. He slammed down knees first and fell flat. Even from her distant spot, the warehouse's exceptional lighting gave Gracie a clear view of his bleeding eyes, nose, mouth, ears …

"We have to help," Gracie said. "I was wrong about them. The situation we were both in on the other side of the wall was shit. It brought out the worst in us. I believed the narrative necessary for us to fight in our war. I hated them for what happened to Dad and Aus. But it's different in here. They don't deserve this, and we can cross the line."

The floating head vanished, and the drones pulled away. A heartbeat bassline throbbed through the place.

"Now"—the man's image might have gone, but his voice remained—"we'll give you five minutes to decide if anyone else wants to cross the line." The lights turned off, throwing the entire warehouse into total darkness save for the spotlight shining on the circle in the centre. "Will anyone make it? Not all the implants work. Do we have a defect amongst our ranks? Is anyone prepared to give it a go to find out?"

Gracie pressed her palm to her mum and dad's wedding rings. "I'm going in."

Matilda nodded. "Me too."

"Shit." Hawk chewed on the inside of his mouth. "I guess that makes three of us, then."

Gracie jumped up and scrambled over the wall, through the gap.

"You don't think there's an easier way?" Hawk said.

Lying across the top of the wall on her stomach, Gracie fought for breath. "There were cameras on the doors." She slipped over, the backs of her feet flailing and slamming against the edge of the roof as she fell. She landed on her side on the internal walkway. Twenty-five feet from the ground. Some kind of spectators' area. Matilda slammed down next to her, and Hawk landed flat-footed with a *crash!*

The walkway had ladders running along it. They'd pulled up all of them, making it impossible for those on the ground to access them. Gracie slid one back down, the crowd parting at the bottom. She climbed into the sea of people. Matilda followed her, and Hawk came down a second later.

Gracie fought her way through the crowd, her friends behind her. Many of the prisoners tried to engage her in conversation, but she kept her lips tight. Anything could happen if she revealed herself as the enemy. Chances were, it would be bad.

Another scream filled the warehouse, but there were too many people between Gracie and the button for her to see. It sounded like someone being boiled alive.

Gracie pushed on, forcing her way through. She rubbed shoulders. Stood on toes. She swallowed back every *excuse me* and *coming through*. She pushed people aside. Shoved some of them. The people continued talking to her. Some shouted. One or two grabbed her, and she snapped away.

Their slow progress got punctuated by the screams of others trying to press the button.

Gracie reached the circle first and froze. Nine dead and bleeding corpses lay scattered around the pedestal. Nine failed attempts. She waited for Matilda and Hawk to catch up. Now in the spotlight's glow, she shrugged at her friends. They nodded in return.

The man's voice echoed in the warehouse. "That's your five minutes up."

Clack-clack-clack-clack ... A metallic winch. The shaking and rattling of chains. Snarling and snapping. Growling and hissing.

Hawk stared up, his jaw hanging loose. "Oh fuck!"

A diseased lowered from the ceiling.

"Like I said, it only takes one." The man's voice. "The warehouse is here to prove the point about vigilance. How vigilance keeps us safe. Because it only takes one."

The diseased spun, turning slow circles while suspended from the chain. It slashed and kicked, writhed and spat. Slow. Inevitable. Gracie and her friends might be immune to the white lines, but they weren't immune to the diseased.

"Fuck!" Hawk spoke beneath his breath. "We're screwed."

CHAPTER 38

Gracie joined her friends. All three crossed the thick white line encircling the button. The ground as slick with blood here because of haemorrhaging bodies, as it had been on the approach to the place with all the decapitations. Every orifice of the fallen seeped blood. A sprawl of leaking corpses.

Whack! Hawk slammed his palm on top of the red button.

Thunk!

Thunk!

Thunk!

Thunk!

All four doors unlocked. Light flooded into the place.

The commentator's smarmy whine rang through the warehouse. "Well, well, looks like we have some more unregistered people in here. This is always a good way to flush them out."

Clack-clack-clack-clack ...

The snarling, snapping diseased was now just feet above the crowd. Almost comical in how it swung and spun like a hanging cat's toy waiting to be batted by a giant paw. Alongside Hawk and Matilda, Gracie fought the tight press of bodies between them and daylight. She shoved and barged her way towards the exit.

The clacking stopped. The diseased remained attached to the chain, but they'd lowered it so it hung close enough to grab those around it. Close enough to be batted away. It hooked a woman and lifted her from her feet. She screamed and kicked as it bit into her shoulder. It dropped her and grabbed someone else, bit them, and dropped them. Too many people in the place. Too many bodies packed into the building. No escape for those within the diseased's reach.

Some turned quicker than others. At least three people already snarled and hissed, possessed with an uncontrollable rage. A lust for destruction. They dived on those nearby. Gracie shoved the people harder. In her mind, she screamed for them to move. But they already had the diseased against them. They couldn't afford to reveal their native tongue too.

Hawk pushed those in front of him.

A similar vigorous approach, Matilda barged and rammed people.

Screams and yells turned into snarls and yowls. The rate of diseased doubled. And doubled. And doubled.

The crowd bottlenecked at each exit. Daylight stretched into the place. Sweat in her eyes, her heart in her throat, her stomach in knots, Gracie yelled with the effort of her attempted escape.

People blocked the doors, the diseased ripping through those behind. Chaos radiated from the creature on the chain. Twenty rows away at first and now fifteen. Why were they stopping?

Hawk reached an open door first. He rammed someone in front of him, knocking her outside.

Gracie and Matilda charged through the gap he'd created

and stepped over the now spasming woman. A white line ran along the ground in the doorway. "Shit!"

Wide eyes stared out at them from pale faces.

"What do we do?" Matilda said.

The crowd in the warehouse grew more animated. A diseased frenzy about to spill out of the doors. The people who remained unturned frowned and cried. Why were Gracie and her friends speaking English?

Gracie shrugged and shook her head. "What can we do?"

"Stay here—" Hawk fought to catch his breath "—and we're dead."

The higher pitch of children's cries spiked amongst the crowd's distress. It raked Gracie's heart, but Hawk had a point.

"Also," Matilda said, "whoever was watching what was going on in there now knows we're not supposed to be here. We showed them that when we pressed the button."

Gracie backed away from the warehouse, her attention divided between the guards' building on their right and the people staring from the warehouse in front of them. "We need to leave."

For the first time, the snarling rage of the diseased overpowered the crowd's cries.

Those at the open gates peered over their shoulders. Some crossed the lines. Their glistening tears turned into crimson tracks. Their legs failed them. One after the other. All the same. All screwed, no matter what option they chose.

The first diseased burst through the doors. It charged with wild abandon. It ran over the corpses of those already fallen. It made it farther than most, but it also fell. Diseased or not, the white line affected it like it affected the others.

A four-wheeled buggy appeared on the other side of the field of severed heads. The rider wore a plain black helmet.

Her long blonde hair rested on her shoulders. She waved for Gracie and the others to come to her.

Gracie said, "You think we should go?"

"She doesn't look like a guard." Hawk turned to Gracie. "And what other choice do we have?"

Several guards charged from the massive block. They shot in their direction. Too far away to be accurate. For now.

Gracie ran, and the others followed. She weaved through the heads on spikes and drew closer to the person on the buggy. Several of the bullets whistled past them. Too close.

The woman on the vehicle said, "Is one of you Matilda?"

Matilda stopped.

"She is." Gracie pointed at her.

"I have William and Olga with me."

"You can take us to them?"

"I can."

Matilda jumped on the back of the vehicle first.

Gracie and Hawk jumped on a second later.

A much better handler of the vehicle than Hawk, the driver spun around and drove off down the main road.

The guards stopped shooting. Why waste the ammo?

A strange device nestled on the handlebars. It had a screen eight inches long and four inches wide. It had several green dots. Gracie pointed at it. "What's that?"

The helmet muffled the woman's reply. "A tracker. It helps me see where the drones and dogs are."

The place was a maze. Gracie's head spun with the rider's twists and turns. She snapped around bends and zipped through plazas. Some of them were filled with people who had just enough time to look up before they were gone again.

They burst from a tighter road, and Gracie said, "What the …?" The guards' block loomed large. "Why are we back here?"

"This is where I live. The guards don't know. I needed to

take you away first so they didn't twig. I'd rather they searched for me miles away." She brought the vehicle to a halt and jumped off. She waved for them to follow. "Come on."

Gracie remained on the vehicle. "And what if we don't?"

"Then you're on your own. And I can't take you to your friends."

Matilda jumped off and ran after the woman, who dragged open a manhole cover, revealing a hole in the ground.

Gracie caught up to them. Daylight shone down the hole, revealing ladder rungs embedded in the wall. Ladder rungs leading to darkness. "How deep is that ho—"

"Quick!" The helmeted woman bounced on the spot and checked behind. "We don't have time to mess around."

Matilda climbed down the ladder first. Hawk followed her.

The gigantic block dominated the skyline. They'd caused too much trouble to be above ground right now. Gracie followed the others, the rough rungs rusty with age.

"Matilda?" Footsteps in the darkness. They came from somewhere deep in this place.

"William?"

"Don't climb dow—"

The scrape of steel over concrete above.

"Wait!" Gracie reached up, but the cover slotted shut, throwing them into darkness. The woman locked the hatch in place. *Thunk!*

"—here," William said.

CHAPTER 39

William's hand throbbed from where he beat against the door. "Let us out!"

Matilda was beside him. She also attacked the steel barrier.

After the crazy woman had locked them underground, they'd searched the place and found a long corridor with the door at the end. "If only we'd been near the bottom of the ladders when you came down here," William said.

"You weren't to know." Matilda slapped an open palm against the door.

Shunk!

A hatch opened in front of them. A letterbox of light. William pressed his face to it. A room on the other side. It had a bank of monitors like Gracie had in Dout, another steel door like the one they were trapped behind, and the woman who'd picked them up. In her fifties, she had blonde hair and an athletic build. Lithe and strong, she had the physique of a survivor. She stood just a few feet away from them.

"Who the fuck are you?" William hit the door again. "And

why have you locked us in here? What's wrong with you, you lunatic?"

"No!" The woman shook as she shouted. She pointed a finger at William. Her pale skin reddened, and she shook her head repeatedly. "Joni's not a lunatic. Joni's the only sane person in this place. Joni's a good person. She's doing her best. She's Mama Bird, making sure she's caring for her hungry babies."

William raised his eyebrows at Matilda.

"Wait a minute." Matilda pointed through the hatch. "I recognise you!"

"Me?" The woman pointed at herself with a bent finger. "I'm Joni."

"Where's Artan, you fucking bitch?"

"Oh, shit!" William said. "Of course."

The woman shrugged. "Artan?"

"Tilly!"

Matilda pressed her face to the open hatch. "Artan, where are you? Are you okay?"

"No, she's mental. She's locked up me and Nick. She says she's caring for us, but she's kept us in separate rooms for the entire time. I've not seen him since I've been down here. I don't know what she's done to him."

"Let us out!" William kicked the door.

Artan echoed his call. "Let us out."

"You fucking nutter." Matilda slapped her palms against the steel. "Open up. Let us out."

The crazy woman clapped her hands to her ears with a loud *clop!* She shook her head and screamed. Veins stood out on her temples. She went off like a siren, wailing on repeat.

After several minutes, the woman finally stopped. Silence in the underground dungeon. She broke it with a soft voice. "Joni's been trying to help. She's been trying to protect you. Joni just wants to make sure you don't die in here like so many others. And were it not for her, you'd be dead already. All of you. The one with the bandages couldn't walk. What if they found him? You in the rat run were being filmed. When you crossed the white line, you blew your cover. You showed them you were different. Same for you three in the warehouse. You don't know this place like I do. You would have all died."

"This place?" William leaned against the cold steel door. "What are you talking about?"

"You don't know?"

"Just talk straight," Matilda said.

"She can't!" Artan shouted from his prison.

"There are so many things you all need to know about this place, and Mama Bird will explain it all if you let her."

William said, "How do we know we can trust you?"

"Because Mama Bird's done nothing but care for you. She's nursed the bandaged one back to health. She's fed both of them. She came and got you all when you were at risk of being killed. She risked her own life getting you out of there."

"She's right," Gracie said. "She did save our lives. There's no chance we would have gotten away without her."

"See!" Joni's finger shook when she pointed at the hatch. "Listen to your friend."

Artan's shout echoed in the cavernous space. "If you've been caring for us, then where's Nick? What have you done with him?"

The woman raised a palm in Artan's direction before balling it into a fist and rapping it against the side of her head. "Of course. Of course. Mama Bird should have done this sooner. Of course." She ran away.

Thunk! A door unlocked.

Artan saw him first. "Nick? You're okay?"

"Of course he's okay." Joni came back into view. Nick ran to Artan's locked door. "Mama Bird looked after him.

Cleaned his wounds. Redressed them. Made him better. You call me crazy, but what would you have done?"

"Then why do you have us all locked up?" Artan said.

"Because Joni doesn't know you. Joni wants to help, but she's trusted the wrong people before, and it's not turned out well. She doesn't want to do the same again. And she locked up you five because she had to get rid of the quad bike she took from the guards. Joni needed to leave you somewhere while she did that. Joni's lived here for years. She can't afford to blow her cover by leaving a vehicle sitting around. Where else will she go if she can't stay here?"

William softened his voice. "Will you let us out now?"

"Can Joni trust you? Do you promise not to hurt her?"

Matilda bared her teeth and breathed through her nose. William eased her away from the hatch. "She's not done us any harm." Gracie and the others shrugged and nodded. They were with him. "Artan, we're going to make that promise. Can you?"

Silence.

A warble of reluctance in her voice, Matilda called through to him. "Artan!"

"*Fine!*" Artan said.

The woman shook and fumbled with the key, tapping it several times against the steel door before she finally slid it into the lock.

Thunk!

The woman jumped back when Matilda flung the door wide and stepped close to her. Joni winced, turned away, and stared at the ground.

William shoved Matilda on. "We promised."

Matilda ran to Artan and Nick. She threw her arms around Nick and then tugged on Artan's door, but it didn't budge.

William pointed at them. "Do you have the keys?"

"Joni's scared of his rage."

William waited for her to make eye contact. "I gave you my word we won't hurt you. I stand by that."

Still trembling, Joni handed over the keys.

"Thank you." William threw them at Matilda.

Thunk! Matilda unlocked Artan's door.

Joni screamed and cowered away when Artan charged towards her.

William stepped between them and slammed Artan's chest with both palms, halting his run and sending him stumbling back. "I believe her intentions are true. Look at how she's helped Nick heal."

His jaw set, his nostrils flared, his brow locked, Artan looked back at Nick.

"She might not have gone about it how you or I would, but I believe she wanted to help. Maybe she can tell us what this place is all about."

"Oh yes." The woman nodded with such vigour William half expected her to rattle. "Joni can do that."

"See."

William pushed Artan away. "Go be with Nick and your sister."

Tears swelled in Artan's eyes. He ran to Nick and threw his arms around him. He stepped back and held his hands. "You're okay?"

"Yeah." Nick nodded. "She's taken good care of me. I'm not fully healed, but I feel much better than I did. She has an ointment that works wonders. She's changed my bandages."

Artan turned to Joni. His eyes tightened, and his voice came out as a weak croak. "Thank you."

Still pressed into the wall, Joni nodded several times.

"Okay." William clapped his hands once. "We've trusted you, and we've not attacked you. Will you help us understand where we are?"

"Oh yes. Joni can do that." She stepped away from the wall. "But not now."

"Stop playing games with us!" Artan said.

William raised a halting hand at him. "If not now, then when?"

"Tonight. Joni will feed you now. You can all rest and be together, and then tonight, Joni will show you what this place is about."

William shrugged at the others. What other choice did they have?

CHAPTER 40

Gracie climbed out of the maintenance hatch after the nutty Joni. Despite her assertions to the contrary, she was certified, a grade A loon. But maybe she could help them. She'd already proven how well she knew this place when she pulled them out of trouble. If they were to remain alive, Joni's experience would come in handy. Even with the baggage of her personality hanging around their necks like a noose.

The wiry woman leaned to one side when she walked. The moon, their only light, shone on her canted silhouette as she led them across the guard block's flat roof, the building larger than some towns in the north.

Tall walls rimmed the roof's perimeter, blocking their view of their surroundings.

"Humans have fought a lot of wars and had many conflicts," Joni said.

"Wha—"

Gracie gripped William's arm, silencing him. Let the nutty woman speak.

"Alliances have been formed and disbanded. Bombs have

been dropped, wiping out hundreds of thousands of people and permanently injuring and poisoning many more. But!" Joni spun around and spread her arms wide while she curtseyed. "That has all stopped. For now. The world used to have hundreds of countries. Areas that belonged to certain groups. Like cities, but larger, and filled with *millions* of people. You're currently on an island that used to be called the United Kingdom. Back when that mattered. You might already know all of this, so stop me if you've heard it before." She let the silence hang. "Now, the area once known as the United Kingdom—" a hard scowl as if she fought to concentrate, Joni raised one, two, and then three fingers "—is one of three superpowers. Three alliances that encompass the world's entire population. We used to be defined by borders, traditions, and many, many languages. Now there are only three. And they're what defines us. We're in the territory that speaks English. We occupy what used to be the United Kingdom, Europe, and Africa."

"How do we know you're not making all of this up?" Gracie said.

"You don't." A wonky grin. "You have to trust me."

"And the other two?"

"The other two what?"

Gracie bit back her reply and inhaled slowly. "Superpowers. The other two superpowers."

"Ah, those little scamps! They have about a third of the planet each. We exist side by side, but not in harmony. One side speaks Mandarin. One side speaks Spanish. As you probably already know. I mean"—Joni leaned close and lowered her voice—"you've tried to speak to them, right?"

Gracie snorted. "That's rarely ended well."

"I'm not surprised." Joni's eyes glazed while she shook her head. "Not surprised at all. We used to travel the world in things called aeroplanes. Vehicles that flew through the sky."

As if they needed a demonstration, she spread her arms wide and ran a figure of eight on the flat roof before continuing forwards. "But we also had missiles." She straightened her arms above her head like someone about to dive into a pool. "They were highly dangerous weapons. They were fired on people and caused catastrophic damage at the press of a button."

The others walked behind Gracie in single file. They would interject should they feel the urge. "Sounds awful."

"Oh, it was. And now, as a result, nothing flies. Anything airborne gets shot down. We still have missiles across the globe, but they're now trained on the sky, ready to detect any aerial danger and"—Joni threw her arms wide—"blow it to smithereens. It's banished the threat of missiles, but it keeps us grounded. Even birds get taken down when they fly too high. The sentry guns take care of that. We have drones and things, but they have height limits they can't exceed."

William caught up to Gracie and Joni. "But there's still no peace between the three superpowers?"

"No. Far from it. There are still wars, but they now fight them on the ground. And we still have our own deterrents should we need to cause damage on a mass scale. No one ever plans on using them, but we're a paranoid species, and it makes us feel powerful to know, if we're going to get wiped out, at least we can attempt to do the same to our enemy."

"What does this part of the world use as their deterrent?"

Joni clapped her hands together in front of her chest. "Oh, sweetie, do you really not know?"

Gracie's palms burned from where she dug her nails in. She relaxed at William's side glance. This woman needed her moment. Listen to what she said and ignore the delivery.

"*You* were the deterrent."

"What are you talking about?" Gracie said.

A burst of laughter surged through Gracie and then died

almost as quickly as it had surfaced. "You really don't know? Why, the north, of course. The diseased. We don't know what the other two superpowers have, but we have the diseased. Should we ever need to, we'll find a way to get those horrible creatures into their territory and watch it rip through them. It only takes one, you know."

Gracie halted. "Where did it come from? The disease?"

"It's left over from a time long ago. A plague ripped through the United Kingdom. As far as the world was concerned, it was contained and destroyed." Joni shook her head like she wanted to dislodge her own eyeballs. "But it wasn't. I mean, how could science allow such a deadly weapon to be eradicated? People kept it alive in secret labs. Almost like the north, but on a smaller scale. They kept enough hosts to make sure it never died."

"So," Gracie said, "our entire lives and struggles have simply been to keep the diseased ready should they ever need to be set loose upon *your* enemies? We existed so you had a weapon in your back pocket? We lost loved ones"—her voice cracked—"many, many loved ones. All so you can have a deterrent?"

"*They* can have a deterrent. They're not *my* enemies. I don't make the call about how things are run in our third of the world."

Matilda said, "If you have the disease, what do the others have?"

Throwing her limp arms up and then letting them fall to her sides again with a slap, Joni shrugged. "Dunno. But hopefully we'll never find out. And whatever it is, it needs to travel on the ground because nothing flies without being shot down."

"You've said that already," Matilda said.

Joni rolled her eyes. "The chances are, it's biological.

Some awful world-ending disease, no doubt kept alive in labs long after it should have been destroyed."

They reached a set of stairs at the end of the building. Joni went up first.

They climbed higher than the roof's walls. Nearly as high as the main wall they'd scaled to get into this place. A similar view to their first, it showed them a labyrinthine sprawl of wide and narrow roads broken up by plazas and open spaces. Residential and industrial, the stark glare from floodlights lit up some parts. White lines everywhere, the lights studding the walls to show when they were safe to cross. Sentry guns sat as larger blemishes dotted throughout the place. Growths on walls and pillars. A reminder of someone else's control. And the wall, the only other thing taller than the guards' block. The *walls* ... Gracie pointed into the distance. "There's another wall?" It stood equally as impressive as the one they'd climbed. "What is this place?"

"It's not obvious?" Joni said.

"Would I be asking if it were?"

"Of course, a Norse horse." Joni rapped her knuckles against the side of her head. "This is where we keep our enemies so we can send them north."

"To keep the disease alive?" Gracie said. "Give it new hosts?"

"Right. We need to keep a high number of diseased should we need them."

Artan stepped forwards. "So this place is a prison?"

Joni grinned and held up her right index finger. "Not just any prison. It's the largest prison in our section of the world. I call it Hell's waiting room."

"It feels like it," Gracie said.

"More importantly," William said, "can you help us escape so we can go farther south?"

"It won't be easy." Joni shook her head. "The guards do a

good job of controlling this place. Also, you need to remember that every prisoner inside these walls hates you either because you speak English, or they see you as their oppressors' kin. Why else would you be here?"

"Nothing about this life has been easy," Matilda said. "Why start now?"

"So," William added, "will you help us?"

Joni paused for several seconds. A range of emotions played out on her features. She finally grinned and nodded. "I've been looking for an excuse to screw him over."

"Is that a yes?" Artan said.

"Yes." Joni nodded again. "Yes, I'll help you escape."

END OF BOOK ELEVEN.

Thank you for reading *Divided:* Book eleven of Beyond These Walls.

***Escape:* Book twelve of Beyond These Walls is now available to order. You can get the book at www.michaelrobertson.co.uk**

Have you checked out *Fury:* Book one in Tales from beyond These Walls? It's a standalone story set in the city of Fury. While it can be read independently of the main Beyond These Walls series, and features new characters, the story occurs at the same time as Between Fury and Fear: Book eight of Beyond These Walls.

If you're yet to read it, go to www.michaelrobertson.co.uk to check out *Fury:* Book one in Tales from Beyond These Walls.

Support The Author

Dear reader, as an independent author I don't have the resources of a huge publisher. If you like my work and would like to see more from me in the future, there are two things you can do to help: leaving a review, and a word-of-mouth referral.

Releasing a book takes many hours and hundreds of dollars. I love to write, and would love to continue to do so. All I ask is that you leave an Amazon review. It shows other readers that you've enjoyed the book and will encourage them to give it a try too. The review can be just one sentence, or as long as you like.

If you've enjoyed Beyond These Walls, you might also enjoy my other post-apocalyptic series. The Alpha Plague: Books 1-8 (The Complete Series) are available now.

The Alpha Plague - Available Now at www.michaelrobertson.co.uk

Or save money by picking up the entire series box set at at www.michaelrobertson.co.uk

ABOUT THE AUTHOR

Like most children born in the seventies, Michael grew up with Star Wars in his life, along with other great stories like Labyrinth, The Neverending Story, and as he grew older, the Alien franchise. An obsessive watcher of movies and consumer of stories, he found his mind wandering to stories of his own.

Those stories had to come out.

He hopes you enjoy reading his work as much as he does creating it.

Contact
www.michaelrobertson.co.uk
subscribers@michaelrobertson.co.uk

ALSO BY MICHAEL ROBERTSON

THE SHADOW ORDER:

The Shadow Order

The First Mission - Book Two of The Shadow Order

The Crimson War - Book Three of The Shadow Order

Eradication - Book Four of The Shadow Order

Fugitive - Book Five of The Shadow Order

Enigma - Book Six of The Shadow Order

Prophecy - Book Seven of The Shadow Order

The Faradis - Book Eight of The Shadow Order

The Complete Shadow Order Box Set - Books 1 - 8

NEON HORIZON:

The Blind Spot - A Science Fiction Thriller - Neon Horizon Book One.

Prime City - A Science Fiction Thriller - Neon Horizon Book Two.

Bounty Hunter - A Science Fiction Thriller - Neon Horizon Book Three.

Connection - A Science Fiction Thriller - Neon Horizon Book Four.

Reunion - A Science Fiction Thriller - Neon Horizon Book Five.

Eight Ways to Kill a Rat - A Science Fiction Thriller - Neon Horizon Book Six.

Neon Horizon - Books 1 - 3 Box Set - A Science Fiction Thriller.

THE ALPHA PLAGUE:

The Alpha Plague: A Post-Apocalyptic Action Thriller

The Alpha Plague 2

The Alpha Plague 3

The Alpha Plague 4

The Alpha Plague 5

The Alpha Plague 6

The Alpha Plague 7

The Alpha Plague 8

The Complete Alpha Plague Box Set - Books 1 - 8

BEYOND THESE WALLS:

Protectors - Book one of Beyond These Walls

National Service - Book two of Beyond These Walls

Retribution - Book three of Beyond These Walls

Collapse - Book four of Beyond These Walls

After Edin - Book five of Beyond These Walls

Three Days - Book six of Beyond These Walls

The Asylum - Book seven of Beyond These Walls

Between Fury and Fear - Book eight of Beyond These Walls

Before the Dawn - Book nine of Beyond These Walls

The Wall - Book ten of Beyond These Walls

Divided - Book eleven of Beyond These Walls

Escape - Book twelve of Beyond These Walls

Beyond These Walls - Books 1 - 6 Box Set

Beyond These Walls - Books 7 - 9 Box Set

TALES FROM BEYOND THESE WALLS:

Fury - Book one of Tales From Beyond These Walls

OFF-KILTER TALES:

The Girl in the Woods - A Ghost's Story - Off-Kilter Tales Book One

Rat Run - A Post-Apocalyptic Tale - Off-Kilter Tales Book Two

Masked - A Psychological Horror

CRASH:

Crash - A Dark Post-Apocalyptic Tale

Crash II: Highrise Hell

Crash III: There's No Place Like Home

Crash IV: Run Free

Crash V: The Final Showdown

NEW REALITY:

New Reality: Truth

New Reality 2: Justice

New Reality 3: Fear

Audiobooks:

CLICK HERE TO VIEW MY FULL AUDIOBOOK LIBRARY.

Printed in Great Britain
by Amazon

44710298R00131